Pascal Garnier was born in Paris in 1949. The prize-winning author of more than sixty books, he remains a leading figure in contemporary French literature, in the tradition of Georges Simenon. He died in 2010.

Jane Aitken is a publisher and translator from the French.

Also by Pascal Garnier:

Pascal Garnier: Gallic Noir Volumes 1, 2 and 3
Low Heights
The Eskimo Solution
Too Close to the Edge
Boxes
The Islanders
The Front Seat Passenger
Moon in a Dead Eye
The A26
How's the Pain?
The Panda Theory

C'est la Vie

C'est la Vie

Pascal Garnier

Translated by Jane Aitken

Gallic Books
London

A Gallic Book

First published in France as *Nul n'est à l'abri du succès* by Zulma
Copyright © Zulma, 2001

English translation copyright © Gallic Books, 2019

First published in Great Britain in 2019 by
Gallic Books, 59 Ebury Street, London, SW1W 0NZ

A CIP record for this book is available from the British Library

ISBN 9781910477762

Typeset in Fournier MT Pro by
Palimpsest Book Production Ltd, Falkirk, Stirlingshire

Printed in the UK by CPI
(CR0 4YY)

I always thought that as long as man
is mortal, he will never be relaxed.
Woody Allen

PROLOGUE
(The way things were)

Damien

'You're sure you can afford them?'

'I've said so, haven't I? We'll take them,' I said to the girl, and to Damien, 'Do you want to keep them on?'

Six hundred francs! Six hundred francs for a pair of trainers, for a pair . . . of plimsolls! I was in shock. I could barely afford to re-sole my decrepit old loafers. But, of course, I kept this to myself and signed the cheque I knew would bounce with the nonchalance of a man who has money to burn. A normal, reasonable father would have managed to avoid buying them, but a sham father like me, who only saw his son every other year, would go to any lengths to persuade himself he was a decent bloke.

Damien, walking along beside me, couldn't take his eyes off the enormous shoes whose laces he had undone because that was the fashion. He wore size 43 and was a good head taller than me. Everything about him was oversized: his nose, his arms, his legs. Time had acted on him like a steamroller, he was all long and flat. He was twenty now. I sensed he was as uncomfortable as I was. All we had in common was a surname, Colombier, and a handful of memories as faded as his jeans. I couldn't for the life of me think of anything to say to him. I would have liked to be rich to make up for this lack. I would have bought him anything – a tree, a dog, a cloud.

'How's your mother?'

'Dunno. OK, I think. I don't see her much, just in passing.'

I was getting a stiff neck from turning to talk to him. An old woman went by, holding the lead of a poor old black-and-white mongrel with one of those plastic cones to prevent it from scratching a pink wound on its back. I felt a bit like that dog.

'Are you hungry? There's quite a good little restaurant near here.'

'I don't mind.'

Damien sniffed disdainfully as he looked at the menu. But it was a good place; one of my editors had brought me here once. Traditional cuisine, but of a high standard.

'Have you decided?'

'*Steak frites.*'

'Wouldn't you rather try something else? The *andouillette* is excellent, and the rabbit in mustard sauce, or the *tripes à la provençale*. That's the chef's speciality – do you know it?'

'No. I don't like things I don't know.'

You can't argue with that. So I didn't press the point, and ordered him *steak frites* and a Coke. While we ate, everything went reasonably smoothly, like the truce between dog and cat at feeding time. Occasionally we stole a glance at each other, both equally astonished to find ourselves face to face like this. I ordered another half-bottle of wine. I felt as if I had a sort of airbag in my chest, about to burst.

'You're not saying much.'

'What would you like me to say?'

'I don't know . . . what you're up to at the moment, your girlfriends. You know, things, about your life.'

'Things are OK. I play in a band; it's going quite well.'

'Really? What kind of music?'

'Grunge; you wouldn't know it.'

'I'd like to come and listen to you sometime.'

'We don't have anywhere to practise any more.'

'Ah . . . Listen, Damien, I wanted to tell you that I'm with someone now, she's called Hélène.'

'Oh.'

'I would like you to meet her. She's a journalist, really nice; I'm sure the two of you will get on well.'

'If you want me to. Can I have a dessert?'

'Of course!'

There was nothing left of the *île flottante* except the sprig of mint stuck to the side of the bowl. I lit my fourth cigarette.

'Can I have one?'

'Help yourself.'

The clouds of smoke between us obscured our view of each other.

'Do you remember when we were boxing in your room and you gave me a bloody nose?'

I saw the ghost of a smile appear fleetingly on his face and his ears reddened. 'It wasn't my fault.'

Damien must have been about eight. I had given him red

boxing gloves for Christmas which made his skinny arms
look like matches. We had stretched washing lines across his
bedroom to make a ring and worn shorts and bathrobes. As
I didn't have any gloves I had wrapped my hands in towels
like a burns victim. To compensate for my height advantage,
I was on my knees. Alice, Damien's mother, banged a
saucepan for a gong. As soon as we began, his fist struck
me full in the face and I spent Christmas Day with cotton
buds in each nostril . . . It's amazing the damage a little kid
can do. But he was the one who was crying, wailing, 'I
haven't killed him, have I, Maman?' He never wanted to go
near those gloves again.

'What made you think of that?'

'I don't know. Here we are on either side of the table.'

'All that's a long time ago.'

'True.'

'I'm going to have to go now.'

Outside on the pavement, we looked ridiculous next to
each other. I stood on tiptoe to kiss him. An old couple
glared at us. I'm sure they took me for a gay man with his
young lover.

'So, uh, bye, and thanks.'

'What for?'

'The trainers, lunch . . .'

'Oh, that. I'll be in touch. See you soon.'

I was in the mood to watch regional TV, or listen to a
Barbara record. I could also have tried to hang myself but
I was sure the rope would break.

Hélène

'It's strange how most human beings are shaped like coffins.'

The man spoke quietly. He was staring at a dozen people huddled together under a bus shelter on the other side of the road. Rain slashed against the café windows. His gaze as he turned to me was obscured by his milk-bottle glasses. 'It's a bit worrying, don't you think?'

Taken by surprise, I shrugged, opening my hands as if setting a bird free. 'C'est la vie!'

'You think so? They say our mortal fate is our mothers' fault. What do you think?'

It was All Saints' Day, or the Day of the Dead in some places. Chrysanthemums bloomed outside florists' shops, and spilled over like harmful algae from the boots of passing cars, which sprayed the pavements with greasy water. Since the morning the city had smelled of damp soil.

'I agree there would be no Day of the Dead without mothers giving us life, but it's a bit facile. They are the first women we kick in the stomach. It's an amusing turn of phrase. Is it yours?'

'No, just something I heard. I buried mine this morning.'

'Sorry to hear that.'

'Don't be. She was an old cow. Anyway, I'll wish you a good day, Monsieur.'

He was, like me, about fifty, with a complexion like a wrung-out dishcloth, and looked as if he were desperate for this interminable day to be over. As he passed in front of my table, he gave off a vague odour of detergent.

Hélène was already half an hour late, which had given me time to turn my receipt into a miniature origami duck. We had separated a month ago and I had to hand back the keys to her apartment.

She arrived just as the waiter was bringing my third beer. She was wearing one of the brightly coloured berets she was so fond of – this one was pistachio green – pulled right down to her eyebrows. Her eyes were shining, the pupils dilated, as her scarlet mouth, like a sea anemone, kissed mine.

'I'm sorry I'm late, Jeff. Someone phoned just as I was leaving.'

'Don't worry, I love hanging around in bistros on All Saints', it's a weakness of mine, yet another one. Before we forget, here are your keys.'

'Thank you. How are you?'

'Like a drowned man at the bottom of a swimming pool without water.'

'Stop acting the martyr! It's not your fault, or mine; these things happen. C'est la vie . . . Why are you laughing?'

'Oh it's nothing, it's just that I said the same thing to someone ten minutes ago. It's a useful expression, about as useful as "the number you have called is not available", or, "the concierge will be right back".'

'There's no point being bitter. Have you found somewhere to live?'

'Yes! A lovely little studio where you can't swing a cat. You put your key in the lock and you break the window. A real little love nest.'

'You're such a pain! At least you won't be able to complain you don't have peace and quiet for writing.'

'True enough, no one is going to come and see me there! Sometimes I have to ask myself to leave, because it's too crowded.'

Hélène raised her eyes to the intricately moulded ceiling and scratched her nose.

'Order me a coffee, I have to go to the Ladies.'

'Fine, off you go and re-powder your nose.'

Everyone has their little habits. You have to put up with them. We had lived together for five years, I with my nose in a glass, she with her nose in powder. Our different ways of anaesthetising ourselves. It wasn't that I blamed her or that she blamed me but we were both upset because we had believed we would make it together. It's not easy to escape the shipwreck of the forties, swimming in a dead sea as thick as pea soup, with that island on the horizon that shrinks as you approach it. We said to each other that we might get there if we stuck together. Our five years together had been nothing but a long suffocation. We had had to bow to the incontrovertible evidence that we would not be growing old together. It was a shame, because I consider old age to be man's noblest conquest, far ahead of horses.

'Wipe your nose, you've got powder on it.'

'Do you want some? It's good.'

'I don't want to feel good.'

Hélène lit a cigarette and swallowed her espresso in one gulp. Already we had run out of things to say to each other.

'How's the book going?'

'It's coming out in September. My editor is very positive about it – he even bought me a hot dinner.'

'I'm sure it will do well.'

'Hmm, we'll see.'

'You have to believe in yourself, for God's sake.'

'Maybe it's for others to believe in me. I'm fed up with writing; I'm giving it up and taking up breeding.'

'Breeding? What are you going to breed?'

'Plugs and sockets. I found a whole pile of them when I moved into the studio. The previous tenant was an electrician. I've married them together and I'm waiting for them to reproduce.'

'One day, I'm sure you'll—'

Her phone buzzed deep inside the enormous shoulder bag she always carried, cutting off her prediction.

'Hello? . . . Yes . . . No . . . I have a lunch . . . This evening, yes . . . (intimate little laugh) . . . Me too . . . Six o'clock . . . Me too, see you this evening.'

Well, 'me too', I'll buy a mobile so I'll be able to leave

myself messages: 'See you this evening, Jeff, don't forget the bread!'

'Sorry, that was . . .'

'Your boyfriend. You should call him back and tell him you are free for lunch.'

'But I thought . . .'

'No, can you see us in a deserted Chinese, on 1 November, listening to the nasal tones of a star from Shanghai and chowing down on spring rolls? Forget it.'

She didn't protest. I paid for our drinks and we parted ways on the pavement, she to the left and me to the right, wishing each other good luck. C'est la vie.

TV

'Why did you do it?'

Serge Cumin, my editor, was looking at me, aghast and open-mouthed as if I'd killed someone, which was sort of true.

Knowing that I was going to be on TV the next day for an important literary prize that I hadn't realised I was going to win, I had spent the previous evening drinking and looking in the mirror. The more I drank, the less I recognised the mottled skin dotted with blackheads, the nostrils filled with thick hair, and eyelids the colour of days-old ham that even the worst convenience store would have hesitated to sell to a blind man. But it was especially the hair that struck me. It was shaggy, like a field of mad weeds with spikes everywhere.

Armed with a pair of nail scissors, I set about taming it. As I chopped off strands here and there I saw myself starting to look more and more like a convict beset with incurable scabies. I only halted the massacre when the U-bend of the basin refused to hold a single hair more. You could see my scalp in places, especially above the ears, as pink as a pig's skin.

'But what did you do it for?'

'I don't know, Serge. I'm frightened, horribly frightened, like when I used to be called up to write on the blackboard in class.'

'Do you think you can do anything about this, Mademoiselle?'

'Impossible, it will all have to be shaved off. But we haven't much time. Perhaps with a bit of hairspray . . .'

'Serge, give me that bottle of whisky . . .'

'No! You've had far too much already!'

'Give it to me or I'll self-destruct in five seconds!'

Against his better judgement he handed over the half-empty bottle and I poured myself a giant shot. A young man with a beard put his head round the door of the dressing room: 'Five minutes, Monsieur Colombier.'

I was always having nightmares like this but usually I woke up from them in the early hours.

'Serge, I can't do this; you go on instead, tell them I'm ill. Make something up . . .'

'I can't do that, you have to go on. Do your best, Mademoiselle.'

The lens of a camera looks very like the hole in a guillotine. I went on set with my scalp showing and my face covered in a layer of brown peanut butter. I was introduced to the other guests, who were all celebrities, but whom I didn't recognise because of an opaque mist that had suddenly descended, obscuring my vision. I shook hands, some dry, some moist. I didn't catch any names; it was as if I were underwater. I was hot, terribly hot. The lights were blinding. I truly wanted to die, to meld into the plastic chair they offered me and to become one with it. It was my only friend and my nails dug into its warm flesh. From the little I could see, my glasses being smudged with fingerprints, everyone was relaxed and I tried to appear likewise by turning a dazzling smile on everyone, my facial muscles fixed for eternity. Then came the signature tune, Rachmaninov. How many times had I heard it, sprawled on my bed, gloating in advance at the disastrous performance of one or other of my fellow writers?

The man with the half-moon spectacles pushed up on his forehead introduced us one by one to the audience. The mention of my name elicited no response from me; I was mummified. None of this had anything to do with me. I was a mere visitor, an extra. I listened, docile, as they spoke an unknown language, which was rather musical, and I laughed when the others laughed. Everything appeared normal. Until:

'Jean-François Colombier, you have just won the prize . . .'

Why was this man talking to me? I had done nothing to him! I was at peace in my semi-coma. I did recognise the book he was displaying to the camera, but what did it have to do with me? Everyone knew that it was a sham. Yes, I had written it, but it wasn't my fault! I was innocent!

'Why do you write?'

(This was the subject of the programme.)

'Because I don't know how to do anything else.'

'And beyond that?'

This man was out to get me. But why? I didn't even know his wife!

Words jostled in my head, pieces of a puzzle whose picture I could not visualise, and which my dry lips were unable to articulate. They emerged as dribbling bubbles. I wanted to vomit, to lock myself inside the nearest toilet. If my words were incomprehensible, my embarrassment and anguish were all too obvious to my fellow authors, who looked away or coughed into their hands, or studied their nails to show their sympathy. All I was trying to say, like a contestant on the most banal game show, was that I was very happy to have won and that I would like to take the opportunity to say hi to my sister, my brother, and especially my mother, who unfortunately had passed away two years ago.

'Good, good. So, let's move on – Pierre Detaille, how did you come to be a writer?'

It was over! My chair was proud of me; we would go far, the two of us. It would take a giant chisel to prise me from it. We loved each other. The people around me were once again speaking that strange language that I didn't know. And I had again adopted the dazzling smile I was sure was going to bring me fame. I was desperate to pee and to have a drink – a proper one this time – and some *choucroute*. It's hungry work being on TV.

'Yes, yes, you were very good! We couldn't quite understand what you were saying, but everyone will put that down to the emotion of the moment. It's good to show emotion, especially for your female readership. You'll see, your sales will go up as a result.'

A little crescent moon swayed in the sky. How I would have loved to curl up in a hammock far away from the noise and hustle. I felt as if my kneecaps were attached the wrong way round or perhaps it was the pavement bending under my every step. My entire body was cramping. What I needed was to soak for several days in a bath of warm oil. I was afraid I would never be able to get rid of the death-head smile that was pasted on my face; it would take a crowbar to unclench my teeth.

I was suddenly rich and famous. From that point on, I would have no right to complain.

Eve

'I really admire what you do, I mean it . . . but the ending of your book . . . how can I put this? . . .'

'It left you wanting more?'

'That's it! But it was good, all the same.'

'I'm flattered; I'll try to do better next time. Who is it for?'

'For me.'

'I'll put "For me"?'

'No! "For Sophie".'

'Right then, "For Sophie, with best wishes . . ."'

For a month now I had been finding I had an incredible number of friends. I had become a sort of literary companion to all the world, whom everyone greeted with open arms even though they usually forgot to close them round my frail shoulders. I let myself be dragged from town to town, as unresisting as a gift-wrapped parcel. My book with its scarlet bellyband opened all doors for me. It wasn't disagreeable, just a tiny bit ridiculous. Overnight, I had become, if not exactly rich, wanting for nothing. Planes, hotels, restaurants were all made available to me for free. The paradox of my new situation was perplexing.

Three weeks ago, when my bank had called me, I could not resist the urge to hang up immediately. Now suddenly, the voice of my bank manager, which had been threatening me for years, had taken on the silky tones of an air hostess. After congratulating me and telling me that he had just bought my book, which unfortunately he had not had the pleasure of reading yet (but that he would certainly read next weekend, by the fire in his country house near Évreux where he would like to invite me as soon as I could make it), he said that he would like to suggest, from one friend to another, some rather interesting investments. I was very touched. To think that all this time I had considered him my official torturer!

'Would you like another drink?'

'I would, thank you. Can I smoke?'

'Normally it's not allowed in the bookshop, but of course, we can make an exception for you. I'll bring your drink and an ashtray.'

I could see the bookseller was smitten, and not just with the number of books I had sold for her. All I had to do was ask politely and I could have what I wanted. I could have asked her to run naked round the block in the storm, shouting, 'I hate literature!' But I didn't abuse my new-found power. My sudden fame had made me a font of wisdom and calm. I wore the condescending smile of those who have made a miraculous recovery. Although I found all the fuss ridiculous, it was rather heart-warming. I was filled with love for everything around me, people, things and animals indiscriminately.

I did not mind signing books, but now my wrist was starting to ache. I took advantage of a slight lull to escape from the crowd. I needed to stretch my legs outside in the unfamiliar town.

No one ever talks about the cosy attraction of provincial towns, the soft glow seeping out through closed shutters as enticing as a red light to a sailor. Say what you like about the middle classes but they certainly know how to do up a house. People only ever visit châteaux, churches and other bastions of oppression. You never see a son et lumière on a housing estate.

I could have lived in that town, I could live anywhere. I always feel at home wherever I am. In fact, I decided to take a piss right there, against a fence, between two cars. I put my tumbler on the bonnet of one of the cars and relieved myself copiously, looking up at the sky, fag in mouth. It wasn't that high up there. I wasn't worried any more about the closeness of the stars. How strange that in the past I had felt they despised me . . . in the past, that's to say a month earlier . . .

Life has so many ways of bringing you down to earth. My flies had just stuck halfway up, trapping my white shirt. 'Damn it!'

I heard a stifled little laugh behind me, the kind actors fear in the theatre. A girl was leaning against the car I had put my glass on. She pretended to cough into her hand.

'It's not funny!'

'I assure you it is.'

'Haven't you anything better to do than spy on people in the street?'

'I apologise, Monsieur Colombier, do excuse me. I was about to drive off but your glass is on my car, so I was waiting . . .'

It had been a long time since I had blushed like that. My ears must have resembled the luminous *tabac* sign.

'It's I who should apologise; I needed a breath of air, and then . . .'

I grabbed my glass, emptied it in one gulp and tossed it over the fence I had just pissed on. The girl looked exactly like the daughter I would never have. She must have been about Damien's age, an Alice in the Cities, as light and supple as the dandelions you blow on to make a wish. I didn't know such girls still existed.

'What are you doing out here in the middle of the night at your age?'

'I'm twenty-five and I came to have my book signed — well, your book, actually.'

'I signed a book for you?'

'Yes, look, "To Eve, with best wishes". That's your signature, isn't it?'

'Yes . . . but there were so many people, I wasn't paying intention, I'm ashamed to say . . .'

'It doesn't matter.'

'No, it doesn't . . .'

She wasn't smiling any more, nor was I. We were looking at one other and between us floated angels I thought no

30

longer existed except on the yellowing religious images of the past. My head felt as if it were made of bronze. A heavy clapper began to swing from one temple to the other and all I could hear was its resonance.

'Your shirt . . .'

'Excuse me?'

'Your shirt, it's sticking out of your trousers.'

'Oh, yes . . .'

The moon was laughing at me as I rummaged in my flies in front of this adorable young woman. I pulled so hard I broke a fingernail but the shirt stayed resolutely trapped.

'This is so stupid, I . . . You couldn't take me to my hotel, could you? It's not far. I can't go back into the bookshop like this!'

'Of course, get in.'

The car smelled of newness, expensive perfume and Craven A. The streets slotted together like the parts of a telescope.

'Which hotel are you staying at?'

'The Univers, I think that's right.'

'Do you know the town?'

'Not at all. I arrived at night and I'll leave at night too. It's always like that.'

'You have to travel a lot?'

'At the moment, yes.'

'That must be interesting.'

'I hate it. I'd like to go home.'

'Where do you live?'

'I don't know. I don't know any more. I don't live. What's Eve backwards?'

'You seem tired.'

'Not at all! Or rather, I'm always tired. That doesn't stop me from living, or at least pretending to live. Tiredness keeps you company like a loyal old dog.'

'Do you like animals?'

'Only snails. Which are a regional speciality here, aren't they?'

'True.'

'Do you know any good restaurants?'

'There are a few.'

'Just give me a moment to change and I'll take you to dinner. Please don't say no.'

'Why do you think I would say no?'

'I don't know . . . You might think I was trying to pick you up, and I'd understand, you know . . .'

'Here's the Univers Hotel. Go and change. I'll wait for you.'

It was good, the Univers, but a bit too big for my liking. It took me an age to find my room.

To Me!

I

'. . . because when you are so afraid of dying, you end up dying of fear.'

I closed the cheap thriller entitled *No One is Safe from Success* that I had just bought at the station kiosk because the title seemed perfect for me. I was one of those people who always read the last sentence of a book first, before reading the rest. For some people, it's the first sentence which determines whether they will read on. The novel began, 'You know, men are like safes, they all have the same numbers but in different combinations.' For others, the judgement is made by closing their eyes, opening the book at random and reading what's there. On page 82 of this one, for example, you could read, 'Agathe, like all women, had her upside and downside, but what he preferred was her downside.'

All readers are satisfied by just three sentences, wherever they choose them. The rest of the sentences serve only to fill an eloquent void, particularly when the book is an 800-page doorstop. What is the point of an author busting a gut to fill up pages when three sentences are enough!

A waiter, his face glazed with boredom, plonked a glass of beer and a limp sandwich in front of me. Foam dripped down the outside of the glass to be absorbed by the Mort Subite beermat. I no more wanted the sandwich and beer than I wanted to read the book. I was only doing what everyone does when they have an hour to kill before catching a train. But time spent in station cafés refuses to be killed. I glanced at my watch. The second hand seemed to be as sluggish as the hour hand. I was used to it. A congenital anxiety, resulting from having a watchmaker father whom death had taken earlier than expected, compelled me from an early age to arrive for meetings a good three-quarters of an hour early. I had spent half of my fifty years of life waiting for a train, or for an official to be free, for love or success or happiness . . .

Waiting is always dull, but I was practised at it and settled almost comfortably into the passive attitude required. I preferred that to running after things – trains, officials, love or success. As for happiness . . . it comes to you when you least expect it, and, because you are not prepared, crushes you as completely as the worst misfortune.

There was only one other person in the café, an old man with his back to me, hunched over a plate of spaghetti, his walking stick hanging on the back of his chair. In front of us a badly tuned TV was showing *The Price is Right*. To the left, above the bar, the predictable football and pétanque flags and trophies were proudly displayed on a dusty shelf above a procession of fake bottles ranging from a magnum of champagne of questionable brand to the pot-bellied Orangina bottle. To the right, the inescapable portrait of

'Marion, 10 years old, missing since . . .' her blue eyes staring out like someone who's just woken up saying, 'Where am I?' No one knew. For years, her photograph had appeared in stations, on the doors of town halls, on street corners, like the pictures of saints handed out to children taking their first communion. Never had 'missing' been so present. Perhaps I had passed her on the street, in a car at a red light, perhaps I had sat next to her in the cinema? How she must have changed since that picture! Anyway, photos never look like the person. All photographs are phoney. All you have to do is open a family album for everyone to exclaim: 'Is that me? No, can't be, how hideous I look!' Because, of course, everyone is beautiful in their own mind.

I didn't recognise myself a year ago, when I saw the picture on the back cover of the book that had won me a prestigious literary prize. I looked dull and stupid. It wasn't like me at all.

The sandwich was so elastic I had to stretch it several inches before I could bite off a mouthful.

'So you're saying 545 francs for this magnificent Limoges tea service? And it actually is . . . 956 francs. Sorry, Anne-Christine!'

The presenter and the contestants on *The Price is Right* were all sporting fake tan and wore blue because it looked good on TV. That's what I had been advised to wear when I went on to collect my prize. I took a swig of beer to erase the painful memory. My performance had been lamentable. The half-bottle of Scotch I had practically downed in one before going on had done nothing to quell my paralysing stage fright. I felt as if I had been poured into a block of concrete. I had gibbered and stammered incomprehensibly in answer to the questions put to me. But still, thanks to the blue suit I had bought the day before (my first suit!), my sales following that appearance had risen considerably. I had rarely felt as humiliated as I did that evening.

'Yes, yes, you were really good! A bit emotional, under-standably, but your female fans will like that; it's appealing.'

I had ended the evening with my head down the toilet at La Coupole.

Who remembers that? Who cares now? I had pocketed the money and everyone had already forgotten me. You stood a better chance of being remembered if you were a missing child than if you were a successful author and I didn't particularly want to be remembered.

Still more than twenty minutes. In two hours, I would be in Paris, and then . . . I wasn't sure what next. I had no plan other than to escape a life that seemed to belong to someone else and to rediscover what I was used to – a more mediocre existence, certainly, but one which suited me, where I had points of reference and felt comfortable. So many things had changed for me in a year.

Glory and money had struck me like lightning because of my book, and love had followed soon after when I met Eve. She was twenty-five, beautiful, gentle, cheerful and miraculous for a man of my age whom two divorces had robbed of any hope of knowing conjugal love again. At first,

I couldn't believe it; it felt like a soap opera: *Love, Glory, Dosh*. A perennial loser does not become a winner overnight. I approached her with caution, believing that at best she was impressed by my celebrity, and at worst was after my money. But then, gradually, I had to accept the truth that Eve loved me and I loved her. She came from a wealthy family so had no money worries, couldn't have cared less about my fame and hadn't read any of my books. Three months after we met, we married and moved into La Châtre, a château she had just inherited from her parents. At first it amused me to sing 'The Internationale' or 'La Butte Rouge', flicking V-signs at the portraits of her ancestors who watched me with a baleful eye as I passed down the long corridors. It felt like revenge for my ancestors, who'd been part of the Commune and the Popular Front. But after two weeks, having put my dirty shoes up on all the valuable furniture and plundered the wine cellar, I grew numb, mired in a gilded dream I could not seem to extricate myself from. Aristocrats possess weapons I was no match for. Now the valuable furniture was mine, the cellar mine, and I started to notice I looked rather like some of the bearded old inhabitants of the golden frames. I was ashamed to admit it, but I was happy.

It had struck me the evening before, after I read something that Sacha Guitry wrote: 'You should always accept happiness.' The cat was purring in front of the fire. Madame Soulié, the cleaning lady, had just left. Eve was singing in the kitchen from where delicious smells of coq au vin wafted.

It was as if time was frozen in a state of absolute perfection that is normally thought of as the state of grace. That was when something leapt in my chest like an animal in a cage. I felt breathless as I put my hand over my heart, fearing that I was about to die of excessive happiness.

'Good God! I've made it!'

Although the red muscle for so long hidden away inside my ribcage had always beaten with the regularity of the Swiss watch on my wrist, I was sure I was about to expire. This ecstasy could only be the prelude to the end, a swan song which would sign my life off with a cruel smile. Happiness for those unused to it is like food for the starving – a little too much can be fatal.

'Jeff, it's ready! . . . But what's wrong, are you ill?'

Eve looked like a guardian angel who had stayed too long in front of the open oven door whereas what I needed was a cold, hard bodyguard.

'No, I'm fine.'

'You're as white as a sheet! Do you want me to call Voisin?'

'No need, I'm probably just coming down with a cold.'

I was sure I was going to die but nothing in the world would make me call Dr Voisin, an old school friend of Eve's who did not bother to hide his contempt for me. We had called him out a couple of months earlier to look at a boil on my left buttock and my memories of his visit were as painful as those of that TV appearance.

'You're bored here, aren't you?'

'No, not at all!'

II

'Papa? What are you doing here?'

'I was passing.'

Damien, who had always had long brown hair, now had a platinum-blond buzz cut.

'Am I disturbing you?'

'No! Come in. Excuse me, I'm on the phone.'

'Can I have a drink? I'm dying of thirst.'

'There should be a beer left in the fridge. Make yourself at home, I'll be right there.'

The sink was buried under several days' worth of encrusted pans and tomato-sauce-stained plates with three or four hardened pasta shells stuck to them. The bin overflowed with jam jars and crumpled biscuit packets sprinkled with coffee grounds. There was a vague smell of silage, or of unclean armpits. My shoes stuck to the floor, making a little pop with every step. I had known dozens of kitchens like this when I'd been Damien's age. It had the same effect on me as the wholesome farmyard smell the city dweller fills his lungs with on his first day on holiday in the country. In the fridge, a piece of Camembert the colour of old ivory languished beside a lettuce heart as crumpled as mine. I closed the door on this polar shipwreck, having extracted from it the last can.

'No, I tell you, I haven't any money left . . . At the end of the week . . . Yes, yes, I'll contact you then. Bye.'

With his head down and his feet up on the arm of a sofa probably retrieved from a skip, Damien finished a conversation it was not hard to interpret. I flopped into an orange armchair probably of the same provenance as the sofa.

'Are you still dealing?'

'Nah, not really, just bits and pieces here and there. It's not easy to make a living from music, I need some extra.'

'Haven't you been receiving my cheques?'

'Yes, but I have expenses. Equipment is expensive, and then there's studio hire . . .'

'I hope you're being careful at least?'

'Of course, I don't want to get hooked again. Don't worry. And how about you, the celebrity? What's become of you? I haven't seen you for ages. How long has it been – a good year, two?'

'Almost. Everything happened so quickly. I only notice time passing when I shave in the morning in front of the mirror.'

'You've put on weight, but it suits you; it gives you gravitas. And congratulations on your prize!'

'Have you read it?'

'You know I never read your books. But I've heard lots of good things about it. And there it is, see, on the table.'

'That's something at least. You can always ring me, you know, or write to me.'

'Well, the same goes for you.'

'I do write to you!'

'True, you write a monthly cheque.'

We were each as uncomfortable as the other. In silence, we watched the zigzagging of a fly that didn't seem to care that it was the beginning of autumn. Damien opened my book, waited until the fly landed in it and closed it again sharply. When he reopened it, there was an extra word bleeding inky blood between two lines.

'Sorry.'

'No matter, literature has to be used for something. If you knew how many of my books act as furniture wedges.'

'Why didn't you ring before you came?'

'I tried to but the line was always engaged.'

'That's because I'm like you, very busy. But that's life! That's what you always said to me when I saw you disappearing out of the door.'

'Perhaps I found it as hard as you did.'

'Don't worry, I didn't have an unhappy childhood. We didn't see each other much but we had a good laugh anyway. And it's in the past now. So, what have you come to do in the big city? Is it for work, a signing, to see your editor?'

'I just needed a change of scene.'

'Life in the château not for you any more?'

'No.'

'You're not telling me you've already split up with . . . what's her name . . . Eve?'

'No, everything's going swimmingly with her.'

'So, what, you're not well?'

'Damien, can I stay here for a few days?'

'Here? With me?'

'Yes.'

'Sorry, I'm not following you. You can afford a four-star hotel, or you could stay with friends and—'

'My friends are old school. They don't allow their kids to take drugs.'

Damien burst out laughing, lit a cigarette and threw his head back, blowing the smoke towards the ceiling.

'You're so weird! You appear, then disappear . . . Oh shit! Excuse me. Hello? Oh, it's you, hang on a sec . . .'

Damien left the room with his mobile. He obviously didn't want me to overhear his conversation. It was a bit annoying, unless he was talking to a girlfriend.

The living room was full of assorted objects all more or less having something to do with music. The latest model of hi-fi (no doubt bought with my last cheque), towering heaps of CDs, primitive percussion instruments, and music magazines and scores scattered here and there like dead leaves on the beige carpet, which thanks to numerous cigarette burns, looked like leopard skin. On the wall there were drawings and paintings like the ones you see in nursery schools and psychiatric hospitals, which slightly covered up the appalling wallpaper with its leafy gold pattern on an almond-green background. A Chinese lantern hung askew from the ceiling on a twisted cord and gave off a murky light. The spicy odour of weed impregnated the curtains and furnishings. The smell was like a Christmas tree, Christmas every day – for bad children.

When I had arrived at Gare Saint-Lazare, I had flipped through my address book, like shuffling cards before a win. But none seemed to fit the bill; there was a sense of déjà vu about them. Behind each of the doors I could knock on (and there were quite a few of them) I knew what I would find, see and hear. Everywhere I would be greeted with open arms, but none would close around me. I had no friends any more, only acquaintances. Damien was neither a friend nor an acquaintance, which was why I chose him, although I could not be sure of finding him at home. I was trying to rediscover my youth, and where better to find it than in the features of that young man who no longer resembled me.

When he came back into the room, my son had the same expression as when he had been naughty at school.

'Is there a problem?'

'No, it's OK. Where were we?'

'I was wondering if I could spend a day or two with you.'

'I think it's a bit weird, but OK, I'd be delighted to have you. The only thing is I have to go to Lille this evening.'

'Oh, that's a shame.'

Damien rubbed his chin, and his head, walked round the sofa, lifted the curtain and looked out of the window. I was obviously an encumbrance, an embarrassment. Youth, by its nature, does not like to stay still. I must have got the wrong address, my youth was not to be found here. My bag looked like an exhausted old dog, the handles like ears on either side of the zip nose. It was an old bag, scarred all over, which had always given me loyal service, but it had had enough. I felt bad for having dragged it out of a well-deserved retirement.

'Don't worry about it, Damien. That's life! Next time.'

'Do you know Lille?'

'Vaguely. I did a book signing there a few years ago at the Furet du Nord bookshop.'

'Why don't you come with me?'

'To Lille?'

'Yes. We can go tonight and come back tomorrow. I have a delivery to make. And we can catch up in the car.'

'You have a car?'

'Someone lent me a car. So, will you come?'

Every fibre in my body was screaming, 'You're too old for this!' but my mouth, which had never learnt to say no, replied, 'Let's do it!'

Damien held out his hand, a watermelon smile on his face. I didn't know if I really wanted to go to Lille; I felt as soft as a half-filled bag, but youth came at a cost.

'If you'd said no, I'd have slung you out, thinking, "Old fart". What do you say to a little line for the road?'

III

I hadn't taken cocaine since . . . since I'd become old. This was of the finest quality. I felt as though a lead weight had been lifted off my head, which, light as a balloon, now seemed to be attached to my body by only the slenderest of threads, which vibrated at the least emotion. Mile after mile, all the junk of rusty memory that had been weighing me down evaporated like condensation swept from side to side by windscreen wipers. Now I could breathe pure air, my nostrils perfectly cleansed, my gums delightfully anaesthetised. The music and the smoke from our joints filled the car with coils of smoke made iridescent by the golden glow of the motorway lights which loomed over us like one-eyed brontosauruses. I felt like I was coming home.

Damien and I talked about music of the past, and of today, and of the future. I criticised some artists and defended others, but it was just to say something, because, when I feel good, I have no discernment, I just love it all — whether it's Mozart, Dalida, Hendrix or Björk, it's all the same to me. Damien, on the other hand, had strong opinions about what was good and what was lousy. I envied him having causes to defend. Because all I had to defend was myself, and not even that every day.

'Come on, you're not going to tell me that Clayderman is good!'

'True, I've never bought any of his records, but one evening — must have been about three in the morning — I wept when I was listening to him on the radio in a hotel in Angers.'

'You were drunk.'

'Undoubtedly, but so what?'

'You can't like everything.'

'Unfortunately, I do.'

'I don't believe you.'

'It's the privilege of age. You can make a fire with any kind of wood; you pick up twigs and you make firewood. As long as it burns . . . you're still alive.'

'But with books, you're not telling me you love them all?'

'Depends on the circumstances. I don't know if you remember the hostages in Lebanon, they were journalists, intellectuals, and all they had to read during their incarceration was an old spy novel, written by an ex-SAS soldier, and you wouldn't believe how much they got out of that book.'

'Of course, when you've no choice . . .'

'I think that's better than having too much choice. Too much choice makes you indolent and capricious, like a spoilt child. So, in summary, I'd say that you can make a world out of anything, but it takes everything to make a world.'

He didn't seem convinced. Good for him; he was at an age when you need certainties. After that we didn't say a word to each other; we looked out at the night with its mysteries, all the childhood fears hidden in the forest, our eyes reflecting the white headlights of the oncoming cars and the red lights of those we overtook, as we disappeared into an uncertain future. From time to time, Damien looked over at me to make sure I was OK. I smiled at him, nodding like the little plush dogs you put on the back shelf. Indicating that of course I was OK; I had been doing this since before he was born. But I was touched by his concern; I liked it when people let me have their seat on the metro, and even when I was younger, I had never minded being looked after, or cosseted. Age was only the collateral damage from life, and there were some advantages. Soon I would be a bit more short-sighted, a bit deafer than I already was and I would be surrounded by caring friends who would make life more comfortable.

'They're quite good, these little cars. Hélène had the same model.'

'Oh.'

I thought I noticed tension on Damien's face. Tiredness, perhaps?

'Yes, it was the same colour; it almost had the same smell . . . the same odour. Did one of your girlfriends lend this to you?'

'Yes, that's right.'

'It's mad, I could have sworn Hélène's was identical.'

'One car's much like another.'

'True.'

'Are you still not driving?'

'No, I don't like cars. They smell, they kill and they make people crazy.'

'How do you manage at La Châtre?'

'I never go out.'

'You let yourself be driven about?'

'Like a parcel, yes. I'm not ashamed of it.'

'Do you still booze all the time?'

'A bit less. I get tired easily. I have wine with meals. She really liked you, Hélène. Have you seen her?'

'I speak to her on the phone occasionally.'

'And your mother? What's the news of your mother?'

'I saw her six months ago and I got a card from her last week. She's dancing in Copenhagen. It seems to be going well.'

'Is she still with her hidalgo?'

'No, the new one is Romanian, a juggler, or a wild-animal tamer, I can't remember which.'

'That's good. They're dependable, Romanians, reliable.'

It was the first time since we had set off that we had talked about the past. Up until then, Damien and I had avoided reminiscing about the good old days, which, generally, are not as good as all that. Now, the ghosts of Hélène and Damien's mother were sitting between us, with the smugness of widows come to claim their share of the inheritance. I was annoyed with myself for breaking the spell which had made the car a no man's land between the past and the future.

Damien stretched his arms on the steering wheel. 'I need to take a piss. We'll stop at the next services.'

In the time it took us to reach the next services, I recalled my first meeting with Alice, Damien's mother. She had been eighteen at the time, and was using the name Dolores del Rio. She had danced flamenco, in her own inimitable style, in the square in Avignon during the festival. I was twenty-three.

I had just written a play called *Petits Fours*, which had been performed in the same square. We had conceived Damien without knowing it, between two rows of vines nearby, under a full moon in July, having mutually sworn that we would each be totally and utterly free of the other. Nine months later, Monsieur and Madame Robuchon, Dolores del Rio's parents, both pharmacists in Fontenay-sous-Bois, insisted that we marry. After two years, there was not a single item of our wedding list we had not hurled at each other. We had been forced to separate for lack of projectiles.

Once parked, Damien hurried out of the car, calling over his shoulder, 'Get me a coffee!'

The ground swayed under my feet. I closed my eyes, spread my arms wide, my head tilted to the sky, under the all-powerful gods, who, at that hour, were dozing on their heavy black clouds. It was understandable; they mustn't be able to see much of the big old green ball from where they were. It was a shame; it was so good to be alive, they should come down and see for themselves now and then, like they used to do in the time of the Greeks. Life was worth nothing, but nothing was worth life, as Dédé said. It was as I was bending down to pick up my lighter that I came face to face with the car's number plate. A number I knew very well for the very good reason that I had paid for half of this damned car three months before my separation from Hélène. I had a little difficulty standing up again; something had locked in my lower back. Now I understood why the gods didn't bother coming down to earth much; they wanted to avoid getting caught up in these family dramas. Even though I had not seen Hélène for some years, I was sure she was still a beautiful woman, and Damien was a charming young man . . .

IV

The fauna of a service station is similar to that found at
the bottom of a ditch: albino shrimps who emerge from
the ladies' loos accompanied by the sound of flushing
toilets, molluscs decked out in leather or quilted nylon
moving clumsily, holding their helmets, amongst the
shelves groaning with silly animal soft toys, dried-out slices
of cake, and compilation cassettes of Alain Barrière or C.
Jérôme. Holding a takeaway cup filled with a liquid whose
only distinguishing feature was that it was boiling hot, I
stared transfixed at the cassette of a virtuoso accordionist,
whose face, resembling a knuckle of ham, was displayed
under the name Vivaldi. The coke and the joints I had used
and abused haloed everything I saw with bright light,
meaning that everyone had a blinding aura. It was as if I
were wearing magnifying glasses. Even if it had been broad
daylight, everything could not have been this clear. I smiled
the silly smile of those who see what others do not – the
smile of idiots, alcoholics, drug addicts and a few rare poets
. . . Hélène and Damien! I had lived with Hélène for six
years, six years in which she had blamed me for my alco-
holism as if it had been a shameful illness, while she snorted

every powder imaginable. She had her principles – alcohol no, drugs yes. She applied a hierarchy to ways of getting high, the way others applied it to society; the remnants, no doubt, of her bourgeois upbringing in the western suburbs. There were drug barons, preferably as hard as nails, and then there were the peasants who bought their poison in shops. She could never understand that I fell into both categories – common as far as the snobs were concerned, but a snob according to most others. She couldn't appreciate that you could fall between two stools, and, even, that you could be comfortable that way. Our microcosm of class warfare had ended in a pitiful nil–nil draw. Damien, with Hélène . . .

Leaning on one of those Formica mushrooms that grow in front of the coffee dispensers, I heard a shrill voice behind me. 'You know, men are like safes, they all have the same numbers but in different combinations.'

The first sentence of *No One is Safe from Success* reached my ears. A midget with arms so short they called to mind the tips of chicken wings was gesticulating in front of a large simple-looking fellow, who had a black eye and one arm in a sling and was hunched over a hot drink. The little man interrupted himself when he saw me turning towards him: 'Don't you agree, Monsieur?'

'Yes, yes, I'm sure you're right. Excuse me, I feel I've read that phrase somewhere recently.'

'Aha! I'll have to ask for royalties.'

The gnome burst into laughter that had the same effect on me as gargling with vinegar.

'Can you believe that this string bean, who has just been run over by a car, is refusing my services? And it's not the first time he's been so silly. When you've drawn the short straw at birth, you have to call on angels like me, don't you think?' The dwarf waggled the fingers that seemed to emerge from his shoulders.

'I know people like him, people who've been given life, but not the user's guide. Who better than me to understand them, to help them? . . . But, no, they insist on believing they can manage all by themselves. What hubris! But . . . hang on, don't I know you?'

'No, I don't think so.'

'Well, let me introduce myself: Monsieur Billot, barrister and thalidomide victim.'

I shook the plump little stump he proffered, not, I must admit, without a frisson of disgust.

'Jean-François . . . Lost.' (It was the first name that came into my head.)

'Lost . . . as in the English word?'

'Yes, if you like.'

'Well, I hope you find your way in all this lot.'

With a gesture of his flipper, he indicated the service station, where at that moment it looked as if insects had been immobilised in resin. Damien appeared.

'I don't fancy coffee any more. Shall we go, Dad?'

The homunculus hopped up and down, while his tall accomplice lowered his head further over his warm coffee.

'Is that your son? *Mon Dieu*, he's handsome! It's enough to make you jealous of the passing of time.'

'Goodbye, Monsieur, pleased to have met you.'

'Wait!'

He twisted over to extract a business card from his pocket, which he held out to me between the index and middle finger of his atrophied hand. 'There's bound to come a day when you have need of someone smaller than yourself. See you again, Monsieur Lost!'

The night was so full of itself that it offered no advice. It contented itself with being blacker than soot.

'What's going on, Monsieur Lost? Who was that dwarf?'

'Nothing's going on. He's a troublemaker, that's all.'

Damien started the car and moved out into a slip road. A lorry passed in a spray of water that gave it cat whiskers.

'Why didn't you tell me this was Hélène's car? I recognised the registration plate.'

'I didn't want to.'

'Are you sleeping with her?'

'I don't want to talk about it, Dad.'

'How long have you been together?'

'What the fuck has it got to do with you?'

'Do you know how old she is?'

'And how much older than Eve are you, twenty-five years? Drop it.'

'You should have spoken to me about it.'

'Why?'

'I don't know, it's a bit incestuous.'

'Don't talk crap.'

'Was it her who called you earlier when I was there?'

'Yes, it was her. We were supposed to go together.'

'To Lille?'

'Yes.'

'Why did you change your mind?'

'I don't know. I see her all the time, I don't see you.'

In the bluey-green light from the street lamps we seemed to float like the yolks of undercooked eggs.

'If I know her, she will have been livid.'

'She was.'

'But you don't care?'

'I do. But I prefer it like this . . . Do you mind?'

'I don't know. It makes me feel a little closer to death. Doesn't it bother you to go where I've been?'

'You didn't leave that much trace.'

'Thanks!'

'I'm sorry, Dad, I didn't know it was going to cause you so much pain.'

'It's not that it's painful. It just . . . pisses me off! That's all. Shall we have another little line?'

V

It must have been ten o'clock by the time we arrived in Lille. Damien seemed to know the city well. He turned the car left and right unerringly, leaving the main roads to go deeper into the narrow streets of the old town. He was like a surgeon manipulating one of those microscopic cameras that light up our insides like Luna Park. Neon signs, blue, green, red and yellow, dripped their light on pavements wavy with greasy drizzle. The more we penetrated into the heart of the city, the more the pulsing of the traffic made the facades of the houses on either side of the little streets expand and contract. I needed to open my window; I felt oppressed, ill at ease.

'Are you all right?'

'Yes, just need some air.'

The fine droplets of vaporised rain on my face helped me to breathe more or less normally. At a red light, the thumping bass coming from a nightclub forced me to close my eyes. I could no longer distinguish outside from inside.

'We'll be there soon.'

'That's just what worries me.'

'Why do you say that? It's a fantastic house, really cool people . . .'

'It's not that. It's the feeling of constantly arriving somewhere I used to be, knowing that it doesn't exist any more.'

'Don't understand. Is it because of Hélène, is that it?'

'No.'

'Don't give me that; you haven't unclenched your jaw
since the service station.'

'It's not that, I tell you. OK, it was a shock, but I'm over
that now. It's not Papa and his kid any more; we're just
people who do what they want, or rather, what they can.
And you haven't said a word since the motorway stop either.'

'We should have discussed it earlier.'

'What for? To dredge up the past, your first teeth, the
start of the school year? What good would that do? We're
all free, totally free, grown up and vaccinated; we make a
big, beautiful family! We should rejoice in that, and yet, how
confining our freedom is!'

'Why are you so bitter? If that's the effect of success, I'd
just as soon stay a loser.'

'You've no idea what it's like to be a loser; you've never
lost anything because you've never had anything to lose.'

'And you're a real pain in the neck, you know that? Do
you? Me, me, me, that's all you think about! What about
others? What's so special about you? You write books, big
deal. You're not the only one. You want to have your cake
and eat it. You're nothing but a big spoilt baby, that's all
you are!'

'That's rich coming from you! You're the one living off
the cheques I send you.'

61

'Stop. You're becoming an old fart and it doesn't suit you.'

I didn't doubt that it was true. I was annoyed with myself for reacting this way because of the affair between Hélène and Damien. It was as if I was being controlled by an oaf I couldn't turn off. I existed with this oaf inside me, we were like cellmates. And now that he had awoken, it was unbearable. 'I'm sorry, Damien, I am behaving like an old fart.'

'No worries, you're letting off steam, we all do that. But don't spoil everything. I'm proud to be your son, I'm happy that you're here.'

I felt a salty tear in the corner of my eye. I bit my lips, remembering that saying of Picasso's: 'It takes a very long time to become young.'

Five minutes later, Damien parked in front of a large black gate like an immense block of chocolate. 'We're here.'

People's silhouettes were outlined on the lemon-yellow blinds of the small-paned windows that lit up the ornate facade of an eighteenth-century town house. The windows vibrated with the binary rhythm of techno music.

'Is it a party?'

'It's always a party here. Old family, old money, but not for much longer.'

A badly shaved guy with a head like an iguana opened the door to us. 'Damien, finally! You took your time!'

'Let me introduce my father.'

'Pleased to meet you. Will you excuse us?'

Damien and his friend disappeared off somewhere, abandoning me in the vast hall of this house that might have been designed by Escher. A marble staircase wound up presumably to a first floor from which drifted some bizarre music that sounded like bed springs creaking under the bouncing of overexcited children. Filled with a dark premonition, I began to climb the stairs which must lead to a sort of scaffold at the foot of which I would certainly lay my head like a hat. A couple of vampires, paler than the moon, passed, staring fixedly at me, while a would-be hippy jostled me, pursued by three or four punks with pink crests. I felt as alone as a child who has joined a new school halfway through the year. I was desperate to find someone to hang out with so I went into a room heaving with people like a teeming aquarium. I felt as if I had been plunged head first into a bin that a dozen maniacs were pounding with pickaxe handles. Some bodies moved like drowning people, while others huddled on worn-out sofas. Thick smoke rendered the darkness almost total. Apart from the music and the clothes, it could have been the 1970s. All that was missing was incense and the anaesthetising chants of a bearded guru. I sat down gingerly on the arm of a sofa, a position that was about as comfortable as strap-hanging on the metro, and lit a cigarette to make me look as though I belonged. I had rarely felt so sad and out of place. That's what death must be like, in the beginning. You think you're still alive but no one pays any attention to you any more. Life is populated with the living dead.

Insouciant youth jiggled about in front of me. The girls were mostly pretty, and the boys too, yet no Lucifer was about to offer me a Faustian pact. All they had was their bodies; the rest was just a badly packed bag of half-baked ideas that would never come to fruition. In ten years, most of them would be nothing but senile thirty-somethings or embittered, prematurely balding employees in suit, tie and striped shirt, stammering banalities to their secretaries, or manual workers exhausting themselves in the Bois de Boulogne in their baggy tracksuits, or liposuctioned women worried about their crows' feet and saggy chins as they explained, of their husbands, that no, they hadn't deserved that. The body was a trick. I could see through them like looking at a medical X-ray; I saw their rusty skeletons pulled by giant strings. I had been wrong to come here; my youth remained intact because it was elsewhere. Not for anything would I go back there. The twenties had never been the wonder years.

'Can I have a cigarette?'

'No.'

'You're holding a packet.'

'Yes, it's my packet.'

'You don't want to give me one?'

'No.'

'You're mean.'

'No, not at all.'

I got up. Behind me, I heard the girl who'd wanted to blag a cigarette say to her friend, 'Talk about an old fart,' and that made me smile.

I was hungry, dying of hunger; I could have eaten an elephant. On the landing, I accosted a tall dark-haired girl bristling with piercings in her ears, eyebrows, nose and tongue.

'Do you know where the kitchen is?'

'In the basement, why?'

'I'm hungry; I want to make chips.'

'Wonderful. Can I have some too?'

VI

In this sort of situation, the kitchen is the only part of the house which bears any resemblance to real life, and that's what I needed as well as a stiff drink. The house was as huge as where I had just been living, but it was gloomier. There were no longer ancestral portraits here, but there were pale marks on the wallpaper, indicating where they had once been. Quite a lot of furniture must also have been sold to judge by the ghostly outlines on the walls and the dents in the carpets. All the splendour of the past must have been transformed into pixie dust by the good services of my magician of a son. All that was missing was a banner across the door, 'Everything must go.' It was probably for the best. Amnesia makes the passage of time easier.

The only remnants of the splendours of yesteryear in the kitchen were the board covered in buttons and indicator lights corresponding to each of the numerous rooms, and a serving hatch now veiled in cobwebs. Other than half a packet of wholegrain rice and a tin of damp salt, I could find nothing to feed myself with. Everything else was liquid – wine, alcohol, water.

'Shit, do these morons never eat anything?'

I dumped the rice into a pan of salted water and waited for it to cook, sitting on a rickety chair, my elbows on the table. The kitchen was so vast it could have housed a hundred Turkish workers armed with their sewing machines. But it was good here, it was calm, it was empty. Empty was good. There were no echoes. The other day, in a taxi, I had passed under one of the blocks of flats at La Défense. Firemen blocked our route. The road was dotted with teddy bears, wooden lorries, pieces of jigsaw puzzle, cubes, multicoloured balls and toys. At the top of the building, a child had had a tantrum and thrown the contents of his bedroom out of the window. Nothing can resist the call of the void, the delicious vertigo.

I opened a bottle of red wine and helped myself to a large glass which I downed in one, then a second and a third, as if that was going to change my situation in any way. I was half a century old and here I was in a deserted kitchen as large as an operating theatre for horses waiting for the rice water to start boiling. Absurd.

'What am I doing here?'

I must have asked myself that question innumerable times and I had never found an answer. Other than, here I am, tra la la, like a refrain. A vision of a tearful Eve stroking the cat in front of the fire brought tears to my eyes. Poor little Penelope. At least Ulysses had been clever, whereas I . . . was burning my rice!

My eyes wet, my nose running, I was trying to prise free some burnt rice when the tall girl with the piercings came into the kitchen. 'Are the chips ready?'

Wiping my nose with one hand, I held out the pan to her.

'You'd have to be pretty starving to eat that.'

She looked even taller now that she was not standing on the stairs. The steel piercing at the tip of her tongue gave her a slight lisp.

'There must be a hell of a din when you pass through airport security.'

'I never travel. I like it where I am.'

'Lucky you.'

She came and sat opposite me on the edge of the table. Her hair was more purple than brown. She had green eyes and wore an oversized black sweater and a skirt so short it was little more than a bandage. She couldn't have been more than twenty.

'Why are you crying?'

'I'm not.'

'Well, you're leaking from every orifice; it's not nice in front of a young lady.'

'Sorry, I thought I was alone.'

'We are never alone, unfortunately. Try and find a spot in the middle of the country to go to the loo. You can be sure that as soon as you pull your pants down, you'll find yourself looking at the ugly mug of a yokel. Solitude, it's the dream of the rich.'

She picked up my glass and finished it. As she crossed her long legs, I caught sight of one of the clips of the suspender belt holding up her stockings.

'I'm Agathe.'

Agathe? *What he preferred was her downside.*

'What's so funny?'

'Nothing, I was thinking about a book.'

'What's it about?'

'I don't know, I haven't read it.'

'Why are you here?'

'I'm Damien's father.'

'The sandman?'

'That must be it.'

'You don't look like him but you remind me of someone. Are you on the telly?'

'No. Would you like some more wine?'

I opened another bottle. She was amusing, this beanpole. Like a puppy playing with a slipper, and the slipper was me.

'I'm sure I know you.'

'Perhaps I'm your father?'

'I don't think so. I can't picture him gobbling down a pan of burnt rice at midnight in a kitchen that wasn't his own.'

'In truth, I'd rather not be your father, or my thoughts would be incestuous. I believe in morality and it would have ruined my life. I'm Jeff.'

'Would you like to?'

'To what?'

'To screw me.'

'Well, maybe I would, but right now what I would like is a big *steak frites*. Do you know anywhere nearby?'

'There are brasseries at the station.'

'Shall we go? I don't know the area, I need a guide.'

Agathe suited her name. Her eyes were like marbles with threads of green, yellow and gold.

'You're old and ugly; you remind me of an old sad dog.'

'Charming!'

'I'll go and get my jacket and we can go.'

I sat on the first step of the stairs waiting for Agathe. The cohort of Lille's finest nightclubbers paraded past me. Nothing had changed since the dawn of time. Since the Lascaux caves. As soon as night falls we still gather together around any vague light, drowning our sorrows in primitive music and intoxicating substances. Man may have learnt how to fly beyond the stars, to walk on the moon, to gorge on the Milky Way, but he still returns to his cave, the fear of the bear deep inside him.

'Jeff! What are you doing here?'

I wasn't all that surprised that Hélène had turned up, lugging a bag bulging like a cow's udder. She had always carried a bag like that, filled with a jumble of completely useless items. Sometimes I wondered if she slept in it. 'I'm waiting for someone. How are you?'

She blinked several times, as if I were a ghost, then stared at me, fixing me with her minuscule pupils. 'You came with Damien?'

'I did.'

'Little bastard! I've come to get my car back. Where is he?'

'Somewhere in there. It's been a while since we saw each other.'

'Four or five years. What a little shit . . . I've come from the station.'

She sat down beside me and, with a toss of her head, flicked back a stray lock of hair. I had often seen her make that gesture when she was annoyed. The soft bag at her feet made me think of those old dogs that you are desperate to keep alive. She still resembled a tall bent white lily, but perhaps it was time to think about changing the water in the vase. She kept scratching her nose and the back of her hands.

'So you know about it?'

'About what?'

'Damien and me.'

'Of course; you have to do something to pass the time in old age.'

She shrugged and cracked a little smile that made her eyes radiate a thousand little sun wrinkles. 'How are you? You've put on weight.'

'Especially round the heart.'

'Seriously, what are you doing here?'

'I needed to get out, to see my son; I don't really know to be honest, an impulse. I don't regret seeing Damien again, I've enjoyed that, but I admit that I feel out of place here.'

'You always feel out of place everywhere.'

'True, and yet I am everywhere, as I'm demonstrating now.'

'You really are an odd bod. But it is nice to see you again. You're not so bad-looking as all that. When are you leaving?'

'Tonight. I'm going to have dinner in town and then take

the first available train. Don't be too annoyed with Damien; I dropped in on him unannounced. We just wanted to take a little trip together. Ah! Here's my guide.'

Agathe wore a black leather coat which made her look like a baby shark. 'Is that your wife?'

'No, my son's. Shall we go?'

'I'm ready.'

'See you soon, Hélène; look after yourself.'

She was looking at us as if through the wrong end of opera glasses, incredulous and distant. 'You never change, do you?'

'I've tried, Hélène, I've tried. Kiss Damien goodbye for me.'

VII

For the first time in a long while, I felt at ease, light-hearted. It was pleasant to let myself be led through the maze of unfamiliar streets by this young giraffe, who was at least a head taller than me. It was a bit like walking with my eyes closed on a beach at low tide. As we moved forward, my memory emptied; I forgot Damien, Hélène, Eve; I became brand new. We are born into the world every day, even if we need forceps to achieve it. There were groups of young people clustered round the doors to bars and clubs. The road seemed to be paved in shining liquorice, splashed with the lights of the city; we were wading through pools of stars. Several times, Agathe greeted people she knew. I envied her; I wanted to belong here as well, to have friends, habits, a house. We crossed a large square that I thought I recognised, but maybe that was in another city . . . I had known so many of these places that I only passed through, long enough to do a signing at a bookshop, or take part in a discussion or a reading at a library. Restaurant, hotel, then the station or airport. They all merged into one after a while, from north to south, from east to west.

'I remember this square. But there was a big wheel, or a roundabout.'

'That must have been Christmas time. So, you know Lille?'

'Not really; I spent probably twenty-four hours here, for work.'

'What do you do?'

'I sell lettuces.'

'Are you making fun of me?'

'No, lettuces, that's all I sell.'

'If you insist. It's all the same to me.'

'And what do you do?'

'Me? I eat lettuces.'

'We should do business together.'

Even at that late hour, the area around the station was swarming with undesirables. Agathe led me to a large crowded brasserie, Les Brasseurs. It smelled of beer, *choucroute* and cigars. After the fresh night air, the heat struck your face like a mask of burning wax. I took my jacket off and rolled my sleeves up before studying the menu. Agathe ordered *flamm-kuchen* and I asked for pork knuckle and a Moselle wine. We might have been in a Breughel painting; we wanted everything twice over. Here, too, Agathe greeted one or two people.

'Do you know everyone?'

'Everyone knows me, there's a difference.'

'How does everyone know you?'

'I help people out here and there. Like you, tonight.'

'You're a tourist guide, is that it?'

'You could say that.'

As our wine was being poured, a bleary-eyed, dishevelled woman in her fifties dripping with gold and pearls came to

74

lean over me. 'Excuse me, are you Jean-François Colombier?
I've read your books and—'

'No, I'm not, you're mistaken, sorry.'

'I apologise, you look just like him. He signed his book
for me last year . . .'

'Anyone can make a mistake. It's not a problem.'

The lady withdrew, stammering more apologies. I turned
my head away, lighting a cigarette, a little embarrassed.
Agathe looked at me, smiling.

'Lettuce-seller, really?'

'Apparently we all have a double somewhere.'

'So we do. Well, here's to ours! Wherever they are!'

It wasn't the first time something like this had happened.
Normally I agreed to sign a corner of a napkin, but this
evening I wanted to be someone else. A good fifteen years
ago, before I had published anything yet, I had dinner with
Hélène and one of her friends, a well-known film star. At the
end of the meal, the waitress, hanging around the table with
the determination of a dog looking for scraps, said clumsily,
'Excuse me, could I have an autograph?' Hélène's friend took
off the dark glasses that made her, since it was dark, about
as anonymous as a fly on a glass of milk, and uncapped her
Montblanc. But it was to me the waitress held out her piece
of paper. 'I can't remember your name, but I saw you on
television.' The star replaced her dark glasses with a bitter
smile, while I signed the first autograph of my life.

'You keep laughing about something without saying what
it is. It's annoying!'

'Personal memories – you wouldn't find them funny.'

'You're right, my memories have never made me laugh.'

Our food arrived. The pork melted in the mouth, a delight! Agathe picked reluctantly at her food, her gaze flitting all over the restaurant. Jean-François Colombier's fan left her table accompanied by two rotund, ruddy-faced men. She blew me a kiss as if to say, 'Your secret's safe with me.' Agathe followed her with her eyes, chin in hand, a contemptuous smile on her lips.

'You should play with girls your own age.'

'That's not very nice. Would you like dessert?'

'Just coffee.'

'Me too. Are you trying to make me believe you're jealous?'

'As if!'

'No, of course not. But I would have liked it. Will you excuse me a minute?'

They were proper beer drinkers' toilets, spacious and clean. You could have relieved yourself of litres and litres, comfortably at ease, legs spread, eyes lost in the expanse of white tiling. I wondered if I was going to screw Agathe. Probably not. For a start, there was nothing to indicate that she would accept, and secondly, I desperately wanted to go home. There's nothing like a little perambulation elsewhere to rekindle a love of home. I'd just had a little wobble, that's all. Now I was back on track. I would fetch my bag, take a hotel for the night and catch the train home in the morning. In Paris, I would buy a present for Eve, an expensive one, and soon I would be back by my fireside, with my cat. That's what I was going to do and perhaps I'd also get a book out of my escapade, a book in which I would sleep with Agathe. I would send Damien a cheque, and a little note to Hélène, and everything would be back to normal, as it had always been before.

When I returned to the table, I found only my jacket on the back of the chair. There was a little note folded and slipped under my glass: 'I paid, thank you, Monsieur Colombier!'

I called the waiter over. 'Yes, the young lady paid, and then left.'

I watched him walk away, perplexed. It was very kind of her to have paid for me but—

'Fuck! The bitch . . .'

Of course, my wallet had disappeared from the inner pocket of my jacket. But what was much worse was that I had no idea whose house Damien had taken me to or where it was. How would I find my way back? The change that I had in my pocket amounted to sixty-five francs, not even enough to get me a hotel room.

In small laughing groups, customers were leaving the brasserie as the staff swept the floor. I found myself out on the pavement with no means of protecting myself from the rain that had started, except to pull up the collar of my jacket. I would be able to find my way back to the big square, but after that? I thought briefly of Tom Thumb. You should never go anywhere without a handful of stones in your pocket.

There was nothing to be done except to walk, cursing everything there was to be cursed on earth as in heaven.

VIII

The rain drumming on my shoulders and the combined effect of the wine and coming down from the cocaine made me feel like a fly trapped in a spider's web. All the streets looked the same. Three times in a row I crossed Grand-Place. The street lamps laughed at the sight of me passing, passing again and almost passing away; the whole city was in fits of laughter. There were fewer and fewer people in the streets and those there were looked at me strangely. I had stepped in a puddle and my right shoe made noises like a sinking boat. I would undoubtedly end up slipping into and drowning in the goddamn shoe. My nose was running; it was starting to be seriously cold. The more I panicked, the more I lost myself in the shroud of stone as if being sucked into quicksand.

Calm, calm . . . I needed to keep a clear head. Why not smoke a cigarette under this porch, for example?

I only had two left, all twisted because I had crumpled the packet in my pocket. I stuck one between my lips, but my empty lighter produced nothing but a couple of sparks.

I chucked it into the gutter, causing a cat sheltering under a car to flee. Even animals were avoiding me. Oh, the beautiful eyes of Agathe! If I could hold her for even a few seconds, how I would grind my heels into those eyes! How gloriously I would strangle her, cut her up into little pieces, pull out her fingernails and teeth and then stuff her into a manhole, hoping that the rats would leave nothing of her but a handful of her dirty red hair!

Imagining all that got me nowhere, but it was satisfying nonetheless.

A bit further on, a neon bar sign showing a buxom blonde with a fishtail was winking at me. The Mermaid. I still had enough money to buy a coffee and a pack of cigarettes. At least I would be able to dry off for a moment. There were a few customers slumped at the bar. They stared at me when I entered, dripping wet.

'A coffee and a packet of Camels.'

'We only have Gitanes.'

'I'll have the Gitanes. And a box of matches! Please.'

The customers ignored me. The presence of a drowned man is never that enticing. As luck would have it, no one recognised me here. It was here I should have happened upon the blonde woman from the brasserie. And how delighted I would have been to identify myself as Jean-François Colombier! I would have told her about my shipwreck and she would have taken me back to her cosy apartment, drawn me a hot bath, poured me a drink and cosseted me like a rare pearl! . . . But here no one knew me; they didn't watch book programmes on television; they probably took me for some homeless guy, not someone you'd want to hang out with. That's the problem with people who have no culture.

As I was desperately searching my pockets for a tissue I discovered the card of the gnome I had bumped into at the motorway services: 'Maître G. Billot, Lawyer, 45 Rue de Paris, 59800 Lille. Tel: 03 . . .'

It was a bit cheeky to call up someone you don't know at two in the morning but . . .

'Can I make a phone call?'

The bartender looked at me as if I had propositioned him. But he did push the telephone that sat on the end of the bar towards me.

'Hello, Maître Billot?'

'Speaking.'

'I'm so sorry to disturb you at such a late hour but—'

'Who is this?'

'Jean-François Colombier.'

'The writer?'

'Yes, we met in a service station on the motorway, today . . .'

'Oh yes! I remember very well. I was sure I recognised you. What's happened?'

'So stupid, I've had my wallet stolen and I'm lost in Lille. I don't know anyone and—'

'Where are you?'

'I don't know. Wait . . . Please, where is this place?'

At the bar, all heads were turned to me, like cows watching a train go by.

'The Mermaid Bar, 33 Grande-Rue.'

'The Mermaid—'

'I heard that; it's five minutes from where I live. I'll give you the entry code. It's on the third floor, the door on the left.'

'Thank you, Maître, thank you very much!'

'My pleasure!'

When I hung up, I felt about a hundred years younger.

'That'll be . . . including the telephone and the cigarettes . . . forty-eight francs.'

After being told how to get to Rue de Paris, I left the bar, my eyes shining with the fervour of one who has seen a miracle. I crossed Grand-Place for a fourth time but now the square seemed splendid with the little square windows of the gabled facades reflecting all the golden hope in the world. They might have been covered in scrunched-up Christmas paper. I had no difficulty finding Rue de Paris; it seemed to offer itself up to me. It's easy to panic but actually life is so simple it's almost unseemly. Number 45 was a 1930s building, its door adorned with wrought-iron Munich roses on a frosted-glass background. I rang, it opened and, spurning the lift, I took the stairs to the third floor four by four. Sometimes lifts break down. *Dring!* And there was Maître Billot letting me in, wearing a dressing gown of wool from the Pyrenees which made him look like Dopey from *Snow White*.

'Maître, I do apologise—'

'No need, come in, quickly. Goodness me, you're soaked!'

The apartment smelled of biscuits, yellowing wallpaper and dust — of which there was a thick velvety layer on all the furniture. It felt as if no windows had been opened since the apartment had been built.

'I won't take you into the office, you'll be more comfortable on the sofa in the sitting room. And, of course, you haven't come for legal advice, have you?'

'No, it's just a silly situation.'

'Like all situations, you must have had a hand in it. Do sit down, please. Would you like a cognac?'

'Oh, uh . . . yes, please, that would be great.'

It was amazing how dexterous he was with his flippers, opening a cupboard, taking out a bottle and two glasses, and putting them on the table.

'Take your time, have a drink and tell me all about it.'

I did. The cognac lit a lovely little fire in my belly, and then I told him my troubles without going too much into the details that would not reflect well on me. When I had finished, the lawyer scratched his ear, tilting his head onto his shoulder.

'A tall brunette, Agathe, you say?'

'That's right; her hair's more purple than brown, but she is called Agathe. Do you know her?'

'I might do.'

Maître Billot jumped as loud thumps on the wall could be heard. As he rose, both he and the armchair let out a sigh . 'You'll have to excuse me a moment. Have a little more brandy, it will warm you up.'

He left the room on that hopeful note. I immediately helped myself to a double slug of alcohol. I always do that when no one is watching and then I swallow half of it in case someone appears suddenly. 'I might do,' he had said. That was lawyer speak for 'Of course I know that little whore.' There was no doubting it, this gnome was an angel in disguise, my guardian angel, the one who had appeared many times during my life, always in different guises, to keep my head above water.

Gradually the warmth stole through me into my heart. I would get my wallet back, catch the first train home in the morning and return to my beloved home where a beautiful young woman awaited me, her eyes red from weeping. Kneeling in front of her, I would swear never to go seeking such mediocre, such risible adventures ever again. Finally, I had learnt wisdom! Later we would laugh about it together as we sipped a good wine. I would promise not to succumb to the lure of my long-dead adolescence.

I could not help smiling as I let myself sink into the folds of the sofa, which called to mind my first fan, Johanna Cheval, a librarian from Saint-Nazaire weighing more than a hundred kilos, who ever since my difficult beginnings had never stopped believing in me. Every month I received twelve-page-long letters which I never read and to which I had never responded. But it is at moments of crisis that you remember your true friends – usually nice weirdos, gentle, loyal and unobtrusive – that the pursuit of some ephemeral glory makes you push far out of sight of your new friends.

Tomorrow I would send her a long letter. I felt a great need for sanctification, for redemption. I wanted to flagellate myself with a handful of nettles so that I would receive beatification, possibly canonisation . . . I was just wondering what my holy shroud would look like when the lawyer reappeared, dressed in a suit.

'Were you asleep?'

'I just dropped off. What's happening?'

'I think I'll be able to get your wallet back. Agathe is one of my . . . clients. Everyone round here knows her. She's a poor girl who I have helped several times to get out of situations like this. If I bring you your papers and your money back, can you assure me you won't press charges?'

'Of course I won't! It's me who looks ridiculous in all this. She has nothing to fear.'

'Wait for me here. Have a nap and when you wake up this will all seem like a bad dream.'

'Maître, I don't know how to thank you.'

'We'll sort that out later. Just give me an hour or so. It's not every day I get to help a celebrity. See you shortly. Have a good rest. See you in an hour, no more.'

After the lawyer left, I had another finger of brandy and two seconds later, I was rediscovering the ample delights of Johanna Cheval.

IX

I cavorted along on her back in the middle of a sort of caravan park or a cemetery half buried in sand. She whinnied and grazed the rare grass of the minuscule little gardens filled with china dwarfs in lawyer suits. Suddenly my mount reared at the sight of a mermaid with red hair emerging from an enormous tin of sardines. Thrown off, I landed in the sand, which changed as I rolled into black flour. In the distance, I saw Damien using a giant spoon to fill bags with sea foam. I couldn't seem to attract his attention – my words were whipped away on the wind like an advertising banner attached to an aeroplane. Eve and Agathe, both naked, ran down the dunes laughing. And then I could not see anything any more; the black flour filled my eyes and gathered at the back of my throat. I was suffocating . . .

Someone was throttling me with a cushion. Still immersed in my idiotic dream, I struggled and with a kick sent everything flying, before finding my feet and standing up. I had trouble keeping my balance; my right cheek was on fire as if it had been scratched by the talons of a bird of prey. My eyes took a while to adjust to reality, which seemed little better than the nightmare I had fought so hard to escape.

An old woman was crawling on the floor squeaking like a mouse. Her claw-like hands opened a drawer and took out an enormous gun that she pointed at me, panting.

'Don't move.'

This was ridiculous. I rubbed my eyes, put my hand on my cheek; it was covered in blood.

'Don't move, I tell you!'

'Madame, there's been a misunderstanding. I'm a client of Maître Billot's, I—'

'Don't say a word!'

I felt as if I were a character in one of the terrible thrillers I wrote early in my career. It was absurd. Astonished, I watched, with my hands up, as the old woman got to her feet, then sat in an armchair opposite me. She was tiny, as fragile as a matchstick model of the Eiffel Tower, which made the weapon she was holding seem even more enormous.

'I assure you, Madame—'

'Shut up! He may invite murderers to my home, but I'm not falling for it. I won't let myself be killed . . . Sit down.'

I sat back down on the sofa, my hands flat on my knees, never taking my eyes off this poor, mad old woman.

'How much has he paid you to kill me?'

'You've got it wrong, Madame, I swear to you—'

'Don't swear in front of him!'

The barrel of the gun veered away to point at a crucifix that hung over the sofa. I sought my salvation in the apologetic look of the large skinned rabbit on its cross.

'I'm Christian, Madame, exactly like you. I repeat that you are mistaken. I arrived in Lille this evening and I had my wallet stolen. I have had to seek Maître Billot's talents as a lawyer in order to—'

'My son, a lawyer? . . .'

She burst out laughing, which had the same effect on me as an anti-personnel mine exploding. Behind the sight of the revolver, once more trained on me, the old woman's rheumy eye seemed to crouch like a rat at the bottom of a hole.

'How much?'

'How much what?'

'How much is my death worth?'

'I have no idea about that! Please, Madame, be reasonable. I have not come to kill you; I've never killed anyone. I'm Jean-François Colombier, a famous writer. Please put the gun down.'

Deciding to end it all, I got up calmly, smiling broadly, my arms outstretched. The bullet grazed my left temple and embedded itself in the left eye of the moustachioed soldier whose life-size portrait hung beside Jesus on the cross. I fell to my knees, head in hands. For an eternal minute, the echo of the detonation bounced between the four walls like a tennis ball. Through my fingers, I saw the woman shaking all over and moving her lips. 'My poor Joseph, what have I done to you? But it's your fault as well . . . Have you ever been married to a sergeant?'

'Me, Madame?'

'Yes, you. Have you been married to a sergeant?'

'No, Madame, I never have.'

'You're lucky. I was, for more than twenty years! No one knows what it was like . . .'

I had imagined many things in my life, but I had to admit I had never envisaged being married to a soldier. She didn't seem to be paying any attention to me now. The gun hung between her knock-knees like useless genitals. Her eyes, brimming with tears, stared at the one-eyed portrait of the officer. I took advantage of this to raise my nose from the carpet which smelled strongly of cat wee.

'Indochina, Algeria, I went everywhere with him, suffered everything . . . the heat and the fevers . . . I looked after him like a saint and then, at Gilbert's birth, when he saw that adorable little monster . . . he abandoned us! Bye-bye, handsome officer! I never heard a word from him after that; he disappeared without trace. The bastard!'

She was about to fire another shot at the portrait when she put her hand on her heart, mouth open like a fish out of water and slid to the ground. The revolver skidded under an old-fashioned dark wooden cupboard.

'My pills . . . My p—'

I hurried over to her and began to shake her without having any clear idea of what that would achieve. She was like a bag of charcoal and just as light. 'Madame, Madame!'

'My pills, in the bathroom . . .'

I followed the direction of her arthritic finger. Bathroom? It was more like a dumping ground for everything and nothing. Apart from the bath, which was filthy, it was like any other loft or cellar. Amongst the mixed jumble of rubbish silting the place up, I spied a bottle on a shelf which had miraculously been spared by the dust.

'Is this it, Madame?'

She nodded, held up three fingers and opened her tooth-less mouth, as dark as the darkest night. I popped in three tablets. The head of the almost dead woman made three trips from the back of her chair to her sunken chest before coming to rest on one shoulder. Her eyes had rolled back in her head but they gradually returned to normal, the eyes of an almost fresh fish.

'Are you feeling better?'

'How much did he give you to kill me?'

'Oh, not that again! Enough! Look, I'm not a killer! I'm a client of your son the lawyer's!'

'Lawyer? That little runt? Did you see any sign on the door?'

'Um, I have to admit I wasn't paying attention. But he gave me his card.'

'Anyone can have a card printed with anything they like on it. If I wanted to I could pass myself off as the Queen of England. It doesn't prove anything.'

'But why?'

The old woman wiped a tear from the corner of her gummy eye. Now she was just a little old lady like any other, like the ones shrivelled up on park benches feeding the pigeons.

'He's playing, Monsieur, he's playing . . . and replaying the nasty trick that life has played on him. He preys on the unlucky; he can spot them a mile off. In that respect, he certainly has talent. As soon as he spots someone in dire straits, this is what he does: he makes them take out insurance. Then he takes them to the edge of the pavement and as soon as a car starts up, he throws them under the wheels. He's the witness, he's seen everything. Then they share the insurance payout. And it works, Monsieur, if only you knew how well it works! . . . Lawyer, him! Can you picture him strutting about a courtroom with those penguin arms?'

Her sardonic laugh was cut short by a coughing fit that doubled her over. I remembered the bloke in the scarf who had been with Billot in the service station.

'It's not true.'

'It is! He's only interested in those who only have their bodies left to sell.'

'But I'm different! I have a profession, I'm famous, I have money and a wife who loves me!'

'I find that hard to believe – he never gets it wrong.'

X

The silence made a deafening noise, a sort of continual blowing sound that shattered your eardrums, like a dentist drilling a tooth with a hole. Madame Billot and I both stared at a point on the carpet midway between us, the eye of a unicorn with ivy and vine leaves twisted around it. The fabric was so worn out that you could see the parquet underneath showing through.

'It's terrible to grow old, terrible . . .'

'You almost killed me just now.'

'I'm sorry, I thought you were a murderer. He brings many here. And . . . Gilbert would really like to see me dead. You see, ever since he's been aware of what he is, he has blamed me, as if it was me that had invented thalidomide! He doesn't love me, he doesn't love himself, he's never wanted to learn to love. His hatred fulfils him. He doesn't need anything else; he feeds it, grooms it, like a domestic pet. I do love him, you know, like a mother, but sometimes I'm frightened, I don't recognise myself any more; hate is contagious. Have you ever despised yourself?'

'Sometimes, but never to that degree.'

'You'll see, everything you have never been, everything

you have forgotten being, is still there, ready to pop up one day like a jack-in-the-box!'

Madame Billot hammered her chest to punctuate her last sentence but nothing popped out other than a hoarse cough that prompted me to grab her wrist for fear that she would injure herself.

'Stop, Madame, you'll do yourself harm.'

'I don't know how to do myself good any more! Will you dance with me?'

'Excuse me?'

'Dance with me; I'll put my record on.'

The old woman jumped out of her chair and trotted over to the cupboard where she took out an ancient record player with a grey tweed cover. She plugged it in, pulled a record from its brown paper sleeve and placed the needle on the black vinyl, which produced a crackling sound, immediately followed by the first strains of 'Roses of Picardy'. She hitched up her nightdress between her thumb and index finger, revealing ankles no thicker than lollipop sticks. She came towards me smiling, her eyes half closed. 'Let's dance . . .'

What else could I do? I took what remained of the little old woman into my arms, just a bundle of bones and nerves held together by nothing but dead memories. Her quavering voice began to sing, 'Roses are shining in Picardy, in the hush of the silver dew, Roses are flowering in Picardy, but there's never a rose like you.'

As utterly ridiculous as the situation was, I could not help being moved by the old-fashioned charm of the music and the old woman dancing. Even the light from the lamp dimmed by a parchment shade seemed to belong to another era.

'You know, I used to be beautiful in days gone by. My name is Liliane but people called me Lili. I had a beautiful life in front of me, as long as a wedding-dress train. In the officers' mess, my husband's friends eyed me up. Oh, if only I had been tempted. I would have made some conquests, I can tell you! But it wasn't my style, I was a well-brought-up girl. It's horrible, you know, to feel like the same Lili, but to be a prisoner inside a wreck of a body. You're too young, you wouldn't understand.'

'I'm fifty!'

'Young, as I said.'

The record was so scratched it was like listening in front of a wood fire. Towards the end, the needle stuck in the last groove . . . 'Tis the rose that I keep in my heart . . . keep in my heart . . . keep in my heart . . .' I tried to break away from Lili but she clung desperately to me. 'No! Let's keep going. Please?'

'Don't you want me to start the record from the beginning?'

'No, you can't! You can't go back to the beginning, it's impossible. Let's go on while there's no end. If you let me go, I'll turn to dust, I know I will.'

'. . . keep in my heart . . . keep in my heart . . . keep in my heart . . .' It was relentless, like a hiccup. I swayed from foot to foot with Lili Billot hanging from my neck, soaking the collar of my shirt with her tears.

XI

I was wondering how to escape this pathetic tableau when the door opened, and Maître Billot appeared, followed by Agathe in a terrible state, her eye swollen and her lip split. The lawyer walked straight over to the record player and snatched the needle off the record, putting a stop to 'keep in my heart . . . keep in my heart . . . keep in my heart . . .' The 'Roses of Picardy' faded away with a noise like a fork scraping an empty plate.

'Maman, you've no business here. Go to bed immediately.'

Wild-eyed, Lili opened and closed her mouth several times as if she wanted to swallow all the air in the room, and left without having uttered a sound, swallowed up by the closing door. I was left standing there, speechless, looking from Agathe's swollen face to Billot's, which resembled one of those sculpted ivory Chinese balls.

'What have you done to her?'

'The question is what did you do to her?'

'What?'

'You didn't tell me the truth about what happened, Monsieur Colombier.'

'What are you talking about, you're crazy!'

'Sit down, calm down.'

'I'm absolutely fine standing up. Well?'

'Well? Well, you omitted to tell me that you had been to Agathe's home, that you had tried to rape her after having hit her repeatedly. You were drunk and high; your son is well known here. In the course of your . . . lovemaking, your wallet fell out of your pocket and—'

'You're making it up! It's a con. And anyway, you're no more a lawyer than I am; your mother informed me. You're a scoundrel!'

'Once again, I'd advise you to calm down, or I'll call the police.'

'I'm the one who'll call them.'

'As you wish.'

He pushed the telephone over to me with his little arm, shaking his head sorrowfully. He was so calm and sure of himself that I didn't know whether to pick up the receiver. I felt shell-shocked by it all – the 'Roses of Picardy', Johanna Cheval, Damien, Eve, the sergeant. I wanted someone to give me an injection so that it would all stop. I had already done several mad things, but now . . . 'Agathe, say something! I won't press charges over my wallet . . .'

Agathe shrugged and carefully inserted a cigarette between her swollen lips. Tears of rage sprang to my eyes. Once, when I was little at school, I had been punished for a theft I hadn't committed and now I was overwhelmed by the same feeling of powerlessness to establish my innocence. It was so unfair that I would end up doubting myself, just in order to cling on to life. In my alcoholic periods occasionally I would lose twenty-four hours and have no recollection of what I had done during that time. But that was not the case here; this bastard was trying to stitch me up.

'You're nothing but a crook! I know about your dirty tricks, the fake accidents, all these poor people you manipulate to get your revenge for being the midget you are!'

'I wouldn't exaggerate, Monsieur Colombier. As things stand, I'd rather be in my position than in yours. And those poor people you speak of with such compassion are certainly closer to me than they are to you. What do you do for them other than make use of them for your novels? Do you pay them royalties? . . . OK, so I'm not a lawyer, but my knowledge of the law is perfect. I couldn't get a law degree because of my disability, so I became a witness, a professional witness for the prosecution!'

'You're trash!'

'So? What dustbin had you crawled out of when you came crying for my help? And Agathe, do you know what kind of rubbish dump she comes from? You know nothing about us and here you're no one. Now it's me writing the script; you're only one of my characters.'

'That's where you're mistaken, Billot. If you had been a writer you would have known that it's the characters who control you, not the other way round.'

'That's enough. You're not on one of your culture programmes now. Let's talk business. Here's what I propose:

a hundred thousand francs and no one will ever know about your acts of abuse and your son's drug dealing.'

'You're out of your mind!'

'You're wrong to take it like that. I was a witness to your attack on this young woman. Your son is a notorious dealer. I only have to say the word and—'

'You've no proof; I'll deny everything!'

'Look at your scratched cheek! And think of *The Barber of Seville*: "Calumniate, calumniate, there will always be something which sticks." An incident like this would ruin your life and the life of your nearest and dearest for years. It's true that I'm an ugly little runt, but if you refuse my offer, I'll never let you forget it wherever you are.'

'I wouldn't bank on it, I have connections!'

'So do I. All these favours I've done in a provincial town. And then Agathe is how she is, but she is very well liked here, including by some very influential people!'

I turned towards her. Salvation could only come from her. 'Agathe, I need an assistant. I could put you up and give you work. You could escape all this!'

'Who do you think you are? I'm not going to be anyone's maid! And why are you suddenly speaking respectfully to me – because you need something from me? Go fuck yourself! Anyway, I don't like working.'

'Agathe, for goodness' sake! He's the one who beat you up, you can't possibly take his side!'

'I'm not taking any sides! Leave me alone! Go and get the money and bugger off!'

A lock of her red hair fell over her eyes like a curtain. No one at home. I could expect nothing more from her. I felt sick. I had never had a very high opinion of humanity, but this was worse than my darkest imaginings. The poor were no better than the rich. There was no more goodies and baddies; everyone was bad. I flopped into a chair, my hands dangling between my legs, my head lowered. 'What you're doing is disgusting.'

'You're not in a position to give any moral lectures, Mr Scribbler. When you act like trash, you find yourself hanging out with trash. Do you think your son has any scruples when he scatters his powder all around?'

'Damien's not a drug pusher! And anyway, where is he?'

'He's where you left him, happy on his little cloud, but if you're not willing to be reasonable, I can promise him a dizzying descent.'

'Scum!'

'For such an important writer, your vocabulary seems rather limited. Come on, a hundred thousand francs and you'll get back your wallet, your offspring and your nice little life. It's not much to pay and you'll have the satisfaction of making Agathe happy. Look at the poor girl – don't you think she deserves her fifty thousand francs? I may be a villain, but I'm fair, fifty–fifty with all my clients! You'd have paid that much to screw her, wouldn't you?'

I had only ever been fishing once in my life. The image of my first fish wriggling about in the keepnet came to mind. I looked at it without daring to touch it. When I could finally bring myself to, the bleak was floating belly up on the pond, dead-eyed.

'I don't have my chequebook.'

'No problem, the banks open at nine.'

'They'll be suspicious if I draw out such a big sum all at once.'

'You think so? Someone as famous as you who has just acquired a masterpiece – this one, for example!' He pointed at Sergeant Billot with the cocktail sausage that passed for his index finger. 'I'll give him to you as a souvenir. I've seen enough of him.'

As the lawyer applauded with one hand against the armrest, I remembered the gun that had pierced the officer's eye. From where he was sitting, Billot would not have been able to see the touching up the painting had received. What I did next was mad and out of character; I was acting as if I were in a novel. I took a few steps towards the cupboard, and, pretending to retie my shoelace, grabbed the gun and pointed it at Billot. 'This is the end! Hand over my wallet!'

The lawyer, his mouth in an 'O' and his little arms raised, looked at me, his eyes popping out of his head. Agathe let her ash fall into her lap. I had never aimed a gun before, apart from a shotgun ages ago. I felt strong, unassailable. The trigger trembled under my finger like a clitoris. I was no longer myself, but someone other, who would know how to extricate me from this affair.

XII

Recovering from the shock, the lawyer rallied. 'I don't think that's a good idea, Monsieur Colombier; it doesn't suit you at all to play cowboys and Indians.'

'My wallet!'

'Obviously, I don't have it on me! Put the weapon down, you look ridiculous.'

'Agathe, tell me where it is. I promise I'll give you your fifty thousand francs, but nothing for him!'

'Don't listen to him, Agathe, he's not one of us, he's faking it.'

Agathe looked like one of the unemployed watching regional news after a heavy beer session. With the tip of her finger, she scratched a scab on her nose.

'Sort it out yourself. I'm tired, I'm off.'

'Agathe!'

I turned to her, brandishing my revolver like the bouquet of a spurned lover. She sighed and rose from her chair, and stubbed her cigarette out on the carpet with the toe of her shoe. She was like seaweed, long and gleaming, a washed-up mermaid. 'You both disgust me equally. I'm not taking anything from either of you.'

As she was about to walk out of the door, it opened, revealing widow Billot dressed all in black, with a veiled hat, holding a suitcase. Agathe recoiled. For a few seconds, time stood still. All the old lady was missing was an hourglass and scythe. The lawyer took advantage of the hiatus to throw himself at me. We rolled on the ground. It was like wrestling with an animal, a pit bull. His little sausage fingers sought my eyes, and his teeth tried to bite the hand holding the gun. He stank of garlic and bad cigars. I could hear his obscene breathing, like a rutting animal, whistling in my ear. I felt as if I were being raped. Close-ups of his skin, his teeth and his hair alternated with views of the chair legs and the fringing on the carpet. Then suddenly the gun went off, deafening us. Billot arched his back, his mouth open. The bullet had pierced the same eye as his father's. Propped on one elbow, out of breath, I saw his body twitching, like ducks that continue to run after their heads have been cut off.

The old woman looked astonished, that was all, astonished. Her vacant gaze went from the body of her son to the revolver that I had just thrown far from me as if it were red hot. My arm was still vibrating all the way up to my shoulder from the shot. The widow calmly picked the gun up as if it were a dead leaf on her parquet. Then she stepped round the body of her son to get to the record player which she plugged in again. Once more the sour notes of 'Roses of Picardy' droned out in the stale air of the room as she took her place in the armchair her son had just quit for ever.

'I wanted to say goodbye to him, but he left before me.

Perhaps it's better that way. I have lived without his love for so long . . .'

On all fours, I was trying to get my breath back. From that position, I had a dog's-eye view of humanity. I saw a pool of blood spreading from a shattered skull, which the unicorn on the carpet was having trouble absorbing. I saw the matchstick ankles of the poor woman swinging in the air, and Agathe's slender legs rising from a pair of bright-red Doc Martens.

'Get up, Jeff, we're leaving!'

'I can't.'

'Get up, damn it!'

I let myself be dragged onto the landing like a rubbish bag the morning after New Year's Eve. The refrain from 'Roses of Picardy' stuttered in my ears . . . 'keep in my heart . . . keep in my heart . . .' Agathe pushed me towards the stairs. It's difficult to walk without knees on legs that are like socks filled with sand. I thought I heard a detonation but perhaps it was the echo of the earlier one. There was no way of knowing. There was no way of knowing anything any more, everything was happening so fast.

The icy air of the night rushed into my lungs, making me cough.

'Hurry up for God's sake!'

'But I killed him. Did I kill him?'

'Serves him right. Shit, walk, will you?'

Someone must have coated everything in tar. It would never be daylight ever again. Agathe put her arm around my shoulders. A shooting pain gripped my chest, stopping me breathing.

'What's wrong with you? You're not going to die on me, are you?'

'I'm OK . . .'

'Hold on to me.'

Agathe's voice seemed to come from a long way off, like someone talking behind glass. When we got to Grand-Place, I had to stop; my legs would carry me no further.

'Try to keep going, we're nearly there.'

'Nearly where?'

The pavement was shiny and undulating like an eel. A group of youths taunted us, thinking we were drunk. You know you can die anywhere but you are still surprised that it will be here and now. Every house front looked like the sole of an enormous shoe about to crush me. What vanity to want to look death in the face . . . I closed my eyes and let myself fall forward onto the ground.

XIII

It was the same night, but everything was white. White walls, white rectangle of window, white shadows that I could see between my eyelashes, spotless white light drenching my pale hands as they lay on the sheet. All that the scene lacked to convince me I was in heaven was an old bearded man surrounded by plump cherubs.

'I've seen cases like this before. You know, when you are so afraid of dying, you end up dying of fear.'

The voice was also white like the odours I could smell. Something, an instinct for preservation perhaps, instructed me not to move. As long as I was inside my body, amongst the mechanics, pistons and cogs that made it function, I felt safe.

'Try to talk to him.'

'Papa, can you hear me?'

I had to make a big effort not to start at the sound of Damien's voice.

'Papa, you've had a stroke; someone found you in the kitchen. Do you remember that?'

No, I didn't remember or rather I didn't want to remember. There were too many things pressing against the door of my memory. The whole world would collapse on top of me if I opened it.

'The doctors say you are out of danger now.'

Poor little Damien. It is life that is the danger. And life was returning to me. A flood of images, each one more incoherent than the last, and in no sensible order, were transforming my brain into a turgid, misshapen cauliflower. So I hadn't arrived? Was I going to have to start again, explaining the whys and wherefores of a world so complicated that God could not find his way around it?

'I don't think it's working. Come back later.'

I heard footsteps receding. Someone knocked into a chair. The returning silence was like a warm bath, a bath of purple ink which I sank back into.

'Move your fingers, Monsieur Colombier. Move your fingers, I know you can . . .'

Talk all you like! Little finger and the eyes, and the mouth, *et la tête, alouette, alouette*! I could also go to the police and turn myself in for having beaten up Agathe and bumped off Billot! I'm not as stupid as all that! As if I didn't know that they were waiting for me in the corridor. Where I am now, no one can get to me. My body is my best hiding place, my safe!

'This makes no sense, Monsieur Colombier. There's nothing wrong with you, all your tests show that. Don't you want to see life? It's beautiful weather today.'

And then? It must be horrible to see a blue sky from behind bars. I prefer a thousand times the security of my inner night. No beginning, no end, it is as blank as the first page rolled into the typewriter carriage. I have never suffered from writer's block. As long as one has nothing to write, one has nothing to fear. It's afterwards that everything is ruined. I can spend hours staring at a blank page; that is the ultimate masterpiece . . . Dear devoted nurse, I would like to obey you, but I know what awaits me when I open my eyes: two policemen and a pair of handcuffs. Your voice, so soft and comforting, is all I need. Besides, one is often disappointed when one discovers the face that goes with a beautiful voice. That happened to me once when I was buying a train ticket over the phone. Seduced by the sensuality of the voice asking me, 'Smoking carriage or non-smoking? First or second class?' one thing led to another and I ended up arranging a meeting. We were supposed to meet in a big café in Paris the next evening at seven o'clock. She was to wear a blue coat and a red scarf. I didn't sleep the night before because I was happily fantasising about the subtle range of her vocal cords. I spotted her as soon as I entered the revolving door of the brasserie. She was so ugly that I let myself be carried right round by the door until I was out on the street again running towards the closest metro station, red-faced with shame. It was one of the most painful memories of my life. Never venture behind the scenes. The green rooms of performers are crammed with terrifying disappointments. Look, I'm the proof, I, who let myself be moved about like a parcel, cleaned, washed and wiped. I am ashamed, I feel pathetic, but it's better than going to prison.

'This is not good, Monsieur Colombier, a gentleman like you . . . Well, I'm going to try to make you presentable anyway; you have a visitor.'

That's how it was. I was visited, like a haunted castle. I didn't move so much as my little finger. I was prepared to do anything to cling on to the little bit of liberty left to me. True, my body was no better than a prison cell, but it was my body; I was alone in it. I didn't allow overcrowding. What frightened me most about prison life was not the solitude — far from it, I was used to that — but the presence of the other prisoners. I prefer being bored on my own rather than in company. I had made my choice. And why were all these living people bothering to come and see me? I should have been dead! It had been so easy to die in Grand-Place in Lille in Agathe's arms . . . What had gone wrong? For heaven's sake, it was as humiliating as receiving a rejection letter from an editor. All that effort for nothing . . . starting again . . . starting again . . . that's not a life! It's not a death either. I had become a closed oyster and I defied anyone to open me!

'Darling, it's me, Eve. Do you recognise me?'

The bastards! They had made her come to the hospital! Even with my eyes closed I could make out her aura, like a cloud of pink talcum powder. They were trying all the right methods to make me crack but it was never going to work. I would hold out, frozen, immobile in my shackles of flesh. I was a rebellious oyster! The Vercingetorix of oysters.

'If you can hear me, darling, raise your hand . . .'

And tell the whole truth, nothing but the truth? I was not going to fall for that. If only I could have told my beautiful love how much I would have liked to jump out of the icy sheets, take her in my arms and cover her in kisses . . . But it was a trap; they were just waiting for me to do that and then they would pounce on me and lock me up! Of course, she was innocent, and did not know that they were everywhere – in the drawer of the bedside table, under the bed, behind the curtains . . . They were spying on me, ready to jump on my first error. How hard it was not to hug her . . . but I could not, no, I could not. I couldn't stand the idea of seeing her through the bars of a visiting room. I could not tell my darling how annoyed I was with myself, for having ruined everything. I did not even have the right to cry.

'Are you sure he can hear me?'

'In theory. Physiologically speaking there is nothing wrong with him. But as for the rest . . .'

'It's in his head?'

'Our psychiatrist will be coming to see him.'

'When?'

'As soon as possible; tomorrow or the day after . . . We're very busy at the moment. I think it will be better if you come back later. If you don't mind, there are some forms to fill out.'

'Of course, of course.'

Who was it who wrote 'Don't shake me, I'm full of tears?' I couldn't remember, but I felt as if I was going to overflow.

XIV

It takes a long time to play dead, almost as long as actually being dead. You go eternally round and round in circles; there's nowhere to go; everywhere's the same. There's not even the possibility of marking the days off on a wall; there is no wall. The menu is always the same, through a feeding tube in my arm, no coffee, no bill. I had to wait for the lights to go off so that I could move about a bit to avoid bedsores and open my eyes on a darkness that was a bit less dark than the inside of my head.

One day at La Châtre, I had set out in the early hours to walk on my own in the fields. The mist was so thick I could not see my hand. I walked along a narrow path. On either side, layers of mist lapped the clods of earth. Seconds seemed like hours. I had become invisible or else the one remaining survivor of a world war, floundering through waves of mustard gas. It was there that I had an intimation of my immortality, of my outrageous resistance to all the bad things that can happen: plague, cholera, falling rocks, falling from a horse, car or plane accidents, prolonged immersion at a depth of two hundred metres – I avoided them all. I roamed the earth like an insistent refrain. I should have been elated but curiously all I felt was a profound melancholy. The countryside was soothing but rather boring. Being the only upright thing moving in a world as flat as that was only mildly entertaining. The silence was so loud I felt deaf. I made myself cough just to prove that I existed, the way you pinch yourself to prove you are not dreaming. It was like a cannon shot. The echo was immediately absorbed by the dense fog so the proof of my existence lasted no more than a quarter of a second. The acrid odour of damp ash reached me. To my left, half a dozen bales of straw were still smouldering, adding their stringy smoke to the grey cotton wool of the sky. I felt, at that moment, convinced that I had reached the end of the world. The reign of nothing at all was about to commence and something told me that it would last a good long while. Of course, I was alive, but afterwards? When there was no more afterwards?

I pissed on the ashes. It was the only thing a human being could do in the circumstances and I went home by the same path. When I got back I made myself a potato omelette.

How much longer would I be able to pretend? Why had Agathe not just let me expire quietly on the asphalt of Grand-Place. Now I was ready and willing. I was just putting off the inevitable . . .

From my bed to the window it was but a step. It would require a little effort to open the window, and another to climb onto the sill . . . My choices were limited – imprisoned with others, imprisoned in my head, or the great eternity. I opted for the last one.

I wrenched the needle out of my arm. Sitting on the side of the bed, my legs like cotton wool, I hesitated. My head was spinning. I breathed deeply several times. Then I went over to the window and opened it wide. The icy air whipped my face, rushed into my throat and robbed me of breath. My instinct was to close the window but I told myself that was stupid. I was ready to commit suicide but I was frightened of the cold? I shrugged my shoulders at that pathetic concern of the living. Right, I was upright; I climbed over the guardrail, facing into the wind, which made the ignominious hospital gown I had been kitted out in flap about my ankles. The sky was yellowish purple, as if bruised, and dotted with little lights – the town in the distance no doubt . . . My last night on earth was just like any other and I was sad about that. I had expected something else, the aurora borealis or a meteor shower . . . I jumped anyway, with no regrets but filled with remorse.

XV

'What on earth are you doing there?'

Dazed, my arse in the damp grass, I blinked in the light of the electric torch trained on my face. My fall had lasted only a fraction of a second, from the first floor to the lawn. The caretaker put his overcoat on my shoulders and helped me up. 'That was stupid, wasn't it? How far did you think you'd get in your gown? You'll catch your death of cold.'

I let myself be led back, docile. I could not even achieve the ridiculous. My walk along the hospital corridors, watched in astonishment by the night staff, was like one of those nightmares where you are naked in the middle of the street. The nurse who looked after me scolded me like a naughty child. She wasn't as ugly as all that, just a little overweight. She put me back into bed and made me take a sedative. 'You disappoint me, Monsieur Colombier, you really do. Don't you know that there are dozens of people here who would love to be in your position? I don't understand it, I don't understand . . .'

And I didn't understand why life and death chose to amuse themselves at my expense, sending me back like a tennis ball. Even under the covers, I could not stop shivering. I sneezed several times in quick succession. Great, I had attempted to end it all and had caught a cold. A snot-nose, that's all I was, a snot-nose that no one wanted. It was with that pitiable realisation that I closed my eyes, lulled to sleep by a sleeping pill.

XVI

'Papa? It's me, Damien. How are you?'

I opened an eye, my eyelid as heavy as a doddery old dinosaur.

'So, what's this I hear about you trying to make the great escape last night? You're incorrigible, you know! One of these days you'll get yourself into real trouble . . . No, shut up! Listen to me; there's someone who wants to speak to you. She's the one who found you in the kitchen, so please don't play dead with her, OK? Right, I'll leave you with her.'

Agathe's face replaced my son's. Her black eye and other bruises were hidden under a thick layer of make-up.

'Hello, you old fart! Well, I look great compared to you. You know, you gave me a fright the other night; I thought you were going to croak on me. Luckily a friend of mine was passing and it was him who helped me get you to safety. Look, I'm not going to go into detail; I hate hospitals, they get me down. I have two presents for you. One is your wallet; I'll slip it under your pillow. I'm sure you won't be surprised that there's not a penny left in it; let's not forget the tip! The second is the newspaper. It's important to keep up with the news, don't you think?'

Agathe spread *La Voix du Nord* out in front of me. The open newspaper looked like closed shutters.

'Can't you read it? OK, I'll read it out to you: "Family drama in Rue de Paris. At midnight on the 11th Madame Billot, a widow, 84, killed her disabled son, 51, before taking her own life. Gilbert Billot, well known to local police . . ." and so on and so on. Understand? You're as pure as the driven snow. What did you say?'

I must have moved my lips, but no sound had emerged. Agathe smiled, which made her swollen lips look like a harelip.

'It's OK, I understood. Keep a low profile from now on. And if you want to make me happy, keep to your world and don't venture out of it any more. I saw your wife; she's waiting for you, behind the door. She's very beautiful . . . Right, I've got to go now. Ciao, old man, I hope I never see you again.'

As she got up I grabbed her wrist. 'Agathe . . .'

'What?'

'If you ever need anything, anything at all . . .'

'You've got a nerve! It's people like you who need people like me; you've got it the wrong way round! There'll be no need for us to communicate again. But you never know, maybe one day I'll be happy, rich, famous and intelligent, and then I'll call you so that you can screw my life up.'

Without caring about her injury, she crushed her mouth against mine and vanished, leaving nothing behind but the certainty she would forget all about me.

An extract from

A Long Way Off

by Pascal Garnier

Translated by Emily Boyce

Published March 2020

ISBN: 9781910477779

Price: £8.99

'I know Agen too!'

The dinner guests span round to stare at Marc with their forks frozen in mid-air. He had surprised himself too. His strange, loud outburst – which was an overstatement in any case, as he had spent barely a few hours in Agen a decade earlier – was the first time he had managed to get a word in all evening, though in all honesty he had had nothing else to say. Several times, in an effort to be polite and civil, he had tried to make a casual quip, to join a conversation, any conversation, but his dining companions seemed to be deaf to his voice. They in turn had nothing to share but profound banalities, but seemed able to at least understand and respond to one another. As Marc dipped in and out of conversations, they began to break down into a senseless brouhaha, mangled fragments of sentences clogging his ears until he could barely make out a single sound. When someone across the table mentioned the town in the south-west, he had grabbed it like a life-raft: 'I know Agen too!'

The hostess coughed into her fist to break the ensuing silence and the dinner resumed to the sound of clinking cutlery, sucking and chewing, forced laughter and incoherent rambling. Until he left, thanking his hostess for a wonderful evening as she gave a strained smile and looked away, he did not utter another word.

The car smelled of a mixture of contradictory scents: pine, lavender, bleach and Maroilles cheese. It was this last odour which had given rise to the others when Chloé had gone through various aerosols in a vain attempt to neutralize the heady aroma of the cheese accidentally left in the boot. Her profile stood out like a transfer stuck to the dark window.

'What on earth made you shout "I know Agen too!" like that?'

'I don't know. I was trying to be friendly.'

'Friendly? Nobody cares that you've been to Agen.'

'No. Me neither.'

'You're being very odd at the moment.'

'Oh. How so?'

'Distant, like you're somewhere else. Is there something on your mind?'

'Not really. Did I embarrass you?'

'No. It's just you shouted so loudly, it was as if you were waking up from a nightmare. Everyone wondered what the matter was.'

'I'm sorry.'

'It's OK. I doubt we'll see them again anyway. They're so bloody boring.'

'You think?'

'Don't you?'

'Maybe. I expect you're right. The langoustines were very good.'

He had spent a good hour looking down at the motorway from the bridge and would probably be there still had it not begun to pour with rain. Often when driving he had seen people perched above main roads like melancholy birds of prey. The sight of them engaged in this sad and usually solitary occupation had always intrigued and sometimes worried him. You could imagine almost anything of them – perhaps they were about to throw themselves off, or their bicycle, since they usually had one propped beside them. What were they looking at? He had vowed to see for himself and was glad to have finally done it. With the roar of engines and the petrol fumes, it was perhaps not as peaceful as, say, watching leaves and twigs being carried along by a river, but it was undoubtedly more exciting. Your head was emptied of thought and the flow of cars put you in a sort of meditative stupor, gradually making you giddy. It must be even lovelier by night, with the headlights. Chloé was wrong. It wasn't he who was somewhere else, but everyone else, all these people speeding out of nowhere only to disappear again in the space of a few seconds, swallowed by the shadowy mouth of the bridge.

He was soaked to the skin when he got home. Since he had no reason to go out again, he put on his still-warm pyjamas, dressing gown and slippers. With nothing to do, he decided to just be. He took up his usual spot on the sofa but felt strangely ill at ease. After five minutes, he moved into an identical position in an armchair. That was not right either. He tried a chair, and another, and another, and finally perched on an uncomfortable footstool housing Chloé's sewing kit. He had never sat here before. The living room looked different from this angle. Though he recognized the furniture, ornaments and pictures on the walls, they looked like copies – very good ones, but imitations all the same. The light coming through the window had changed too, turning the sofa a very slightly different shape and colour. It was as if the whole room were in flux.

Without thinking, he picked up the magnifying glass Chloé used to count embroidery stitches and inspected the palm of his hand. In the absence of a future he saw a fragment of his past, a small V-shaped scar caused by cutting his hand on a broken window at the age of seven. Then he studied the stripes of his pyjamas, stretched taut over his knees, followed by the cracked leather soles of his slippers. To think people went to the trouble of climbing mountains to look down on the world, when a magnifying glass did exactly the same thing.

He kept the house reasonably tidy, regularly vacuuming and passing round the duster, but it was astonishing what you could find hidden between the threads of the rug – tiny crumbs, fine fibres, hairs from body and head, particles of more or less identifiable materials which took on extraordinary proportions through the convex lens of the magnifying glass. It would take days on end to cover this pseudo-Persian expanse, with patterns evoking everything from turbulent rivers to tropical forests and arid deserts. As he crawled over the carpet, he had the powerful sense of returning from a very long journey. It was his childhood he was tracing, filigreed in the intricate swirls of the carpet. He saw it surge from the thread like a spring gushing through a clump of watercress. When exactly had he lost it? We wake up one day and all our toys, so magical and full of life only yesterday, have become inert, futile, useless objects . . .

'What on earth are you doing crawling about on the floor? Have you lost something?'

'Yes . . . no. I wasn't expecting you till later.'

'I managed to get out early. You're already in your pyjamas?'

'I felt a bit under the weather this morning. I haven't been out.'

'Have you called the doctor?'

'No, I took an aspirin. I feel OK now.'

'You still haven't had the flu jab, have you?'

'I'll go next week, I promise.'

'You really should. Now you're over sixty . . . Especially in this weather. Everyone in the office has got a cold, it's a hotbed for germs. I'm drenched. I think I'll have a nice hot bath.'

'Shall I make some onion soup for dinner?'
'Good idea.'

The onions were browning in sizzling butter. He poured in a glass of white wine, added water, salt and pepper, turned down the heat and covered the pan. He was dying to tell Chloé about his amazing experience on the motorway bridge, and how he had rediscovered his childhood amid the patterns of the carpet. But would she understand? No, she would be concerned. He would have to explain. It would take hours, and even then . . . It was school that had taught him to hide away. From the first day, he had realized he would have two lives, his outward existence and the inner one he could never share. Chloé appeared with a towel wrapped in a turban around her head.

'Mmm, that smells good!'

She looked so beautiful with the bath steam rising off her skin. Why couldn't he tell her about the bridge and the rug? Tears formed in his eyes.

'What's the matter, darling? Why are you crying?'

'It's the onions.'

'Sure? Not even a glass?'

'No, thank you.'

'Suit yourself. Now, where was I? . . . Oh, yes! So, Elsa fucked off on that fateful 11th September and thanks to those bastard terrorists I couldn't even complain about it. Collateral damage, you might say.'

Marc was no longer listening. He saw the words coming out of those fat, tomato sauce-covered lips reminiscent of two slugs coupling, but could not make sense of them. The hideous mouth chewed sentences and expelled them like droppings. The brasserie was nauseatingly hot, the air filled with a suffocating blend of *choucroute*, fish, cigar smoke, snatches of conversation, laughter and waiters shouting orders into the kitchen, the atmosphere so thick you could almost slice it. Looking out through misted, half-curtained windows, he could see umbrellas passing on the grey-blue street.

'Could you excuse me a minute?'

The stairs leading to the toilets seemed to descend endlessly into the bowels of the restaurant. While he waited his turn, Marc washed his hands. The water was lukewarm and smelled bad. His hair was slicked to his forehead with sweat. The toilet flushed and the door opened.

'Sorry, excuse me.'

'It's fine.'

He couldn't tell if it was a man, woman or bear who had emerged from the cubicle. He went in, pushed the bolt across and sat down. His hands were shaking on his knees. Despite breathing through his mouth, he could not avoid the wafts of detergent, piss and shit seeping under his clothes and through his skin.

Get out, now!

He pulled the chain, raced back upstairs holding his breath, grabbed his anorak from the coat stand and slipped out of the brasserie like a thief. Not until he was two streets away could he breathe normally again. He was not sure what he had just escaped from.

What would Claude think of him? You couldn't just ditch a friend who had invited you out to lunch. Never mind, he would call him this evening, or tomorrow, or the day after tomorrow. Maybe never.

The roads seemed to be tangled together in a complex mesh, apparently leading nowhere. All that could be said of them was that they had two ends and could be passed in both directions. Each had a more attractive side with neon shop lights spilling onto the wet pavement. He stopped in front of a pet shop selling dogs, cats, rats and birds. Through the window, half a dozen dishevelled-looking kittens were squirming about in straw-lined cages. Some were scratching their ears, others licking their own arseholes, but none were smiling. He found himself drawn to a particularly fat, fluffy and sluggish cat, whose eyes remained closed and ears flat while the little ones climbed all over him and squabbled in his face. Such exemplary indifference made him the ideal travelling companion for a journey into the abyss.

The shop had a circus aroma of damp, hot cat litter, a bit like the brasserie. The silence was filled with cooing, rustling wings, yowling and yapping.

'Can I help you?'

'I'd like that fat cat in the corner, the one sleeping under all the others.'

'This one?'

'Yes.'

'The thing is . . . he's getting on a bit. He had an accident. I held onto him . . . out of kindness.'

'That's the one I want.'

The woman reached into the cage to pull out the animal, who still did not wake up, and placed him in his hands. He was soft and warm, proof that he was not dead.

'All our animals are vaccinated and chipped. Even him.'

The cat deigned to raise an eyelid, darting a slit of green towards the hand that stroked him, yawned to reveal a largely toothless jaw, and curled up again, as if to say, 'It's all the same to me.'

'I'll take him.'

On the metro, the plaintive meows emerging from the

cage drew tender glances from female passengers. Marc knew he had made the right choice.

'You bought it?'
  'Well, yes.'
  'Were you looking for one?'
  'Not especially. Let's just say we had a meeting of minds. Are you annoyed?'
  'No, it's just . . . a bit surprising. He's very fat. What shall we call him?'
  He had not thought about that. People gave animals such stupid names, by and large.
  'I don't know. Do we have to name him?'
  'Of course! Has he had anything to eat?'
  'Not yet.'
  'I'll get him something. Come here, little chap.'

'*Today, I bought a cat.*'